The **Love** That Lies Between Us

Stories of Love Vol I

Stacey Covington-Lee

STACEY COVINGTON-LEE

ISBN – 978-0-692-98322-5

Published by: SCL Novel Publications

Edited by: Queen Lit Publications for Allyson Edits

Formatting/Typesetting: Allyson Edits

Book Cover: Firstborn Designs

Printed in the United States

DEDICATION

This book is dedicated to my forever friend, my "ride or die," Cassandra Renee Smith, my older sister, T'Irma (Sister) Covington, and my beautiful mother, Myrtice Covington. Cassandra, you pushed me to use my gift, follow my dream of writing, and you encouraged me every step of the way. T'Irma, I'm writing these stories on behalf of both of us and soon I'll tell your story. Mother, your constant encouragement means the world to me. I know you can't read my work independently anymore, but it tickles me pink to know that you force your nurses to read my stories to you. I know you say you love me more, but I will always love you the most.

Rest in sweet peace, Cassandra and Sister

ACKNOWLEDGMENTS

To God be the Glory! I thank Him for the very air that I breathe. Everyone does not recognize their God given gifts early in life, but I thank Him for revealing mine and giving me the desire to begin my writing journey so early. Like so many, I started on my pre-destined path, but veered off for far too long. However, it was His grace that pulled me back, gave me the vision, and let me know that I was capable of more, that I was deserving of more. Thank you, God, not only for the words, but for every blessing that you have delivered. My life belongs to you!

Laugh all you want, but yes, little ole me has an entourage. My husband and my son have never wavered in their support for me. They spread the word, share my work, and hit the road with me to do this book thing. Ken and Joshua, thank you guys for loving me enough to support me in making my dreams come true. My mother, Myrtice Covington, is a continuous source of love and encouragement. Mother, I thank you, I appreciate you, and I love you. To my friends that have supported me throughout this journey, I say thank you. My circle may be small, but it is mighty!

When I think about the readers, bloggers, reviewers, and radio hosts that have supported me over the years, my heart gets full. To write is amazing, but to write and have people read it, review it, and promote it, well that's a dream come true. Readers, bloggers, reviewers, and hosts, I don't take your support for granted. I appreciate it and will forever be grateful for it. Thank you, thank you, thank you!

To every author and publisher that has shared knowledge, imparted wisdom, and helped to make me better, I say thank you. In the words of Bernie Mac, "There's room at the cross for all of us" and I'm grateful to those that understand that.

TABLE OF CONTENTS

Loving Myself Enough to Know

The Longest Hour

Nelson finished his breakfast and pushed back from the table. He headed for the front door and was pleased to see his dutiful wife, Robin, standing there with his briefcase in hand.

"That's my girl. Breakfast was good and on time and you're standing here to give me a proper send off. It took some time, but you're finally learning. I don't know what took you so long, but I'm glad you've finally learned. I won't be late. I want lasagna for dinner, have it on the table when I get here."

He leaned in for a kiss, but Robin unconsciously flinched. Nelson looked at her angrily, roughly grabbed her face in his hand and squeezed before planting a kiss on her lips. He released his grip and walked out the door. Robin turned the lock and cursed his name as the taste of blood dripped from the inside of her cheek to her tongue.

Robin rinsed her mouth and poured herself a cup of coffee. This was her time to relax and plan her escape. Six years ago, when she married Nelson, she thought she'd hit the jackpot. A successful business man that wanted to take care of her, what woman wouldn't want that? In return, all she had to do was maintain a clean house and prepare their meals. She didn't realize that Nelson's version of a clean house meant that nothing could ever be out of place and a speck of dust should never exist within those four walls. At first, she thought he was being silly, joking around, but the cracked rib let her know that he was as serious as sin. But Robin was serious too and fought back. She scratched and clawed him like she was in the fight of her life. When she woke up hours later, still sprawled out on the floor, she knew that she was in fact going to have to fight for her life.

Over the years, she'd tried to leave multiple times, but he controlled the money. He had isolated her from her family and friends, and ultimately threatened the life of their unborn child. She was stuck. But after the late term loss of their baby, Robin began to concoct a plan. She started swiping small amounts of money, collecting change, and pawned old jewelry. Over the course of four years, she'd managed to save $1,500, enough to get her back to Houston, back to her family. Robin was waiting for Nelson's next business trip. While he was away, she'd pack the necessities and leave.

Robin had cleaned the house, placed dinner in the oven, and looked at the clock. Nelson would be home in an hour. The five o'clock hour was always the longest. It was the hour that her heart filled with fear, her soul with dread. It was the hour before Nelson returned home. She anxiously ran around the house making sure everything was in its place and that she looked presentable. With only ten minutes until Nelson's return, Robin grabbed her serrated knife and began slicing the garlic bread. The oven beeped, signaling that the lasagna was done. She grabbed the oven mitts, removed the dish, and turned to place it on the counter. Unfortunately, Nelson came home five minutes early. Robin was dishing up the food when Nelson walked into the kitchen.

"Why isn't dinner on the table?"

"You're a couple of minutes early, but I'm plating it now, sweetheart."

"So, it's my fault that your ignorant ass doesn't have dinner ready?" He barked as he slapped her across the back of the head.

Robin started to answer, but quickly changed her mind. Nothing she said would be right.

"Answer me!" He screamed as he spun her around and smacked her in the mouth. He was unmoved by her cut lip or the stream of blood that oozed from it. But still, Robin remained silent.

"I'm working hard to make a good life for you and you can't even have dinner on the table when I get home? You stupid bitch!"

Another punch landed at the corner of her eye and Robin saw stars. She grabbed the counter to keep from falling. As he ranted and raved, something told her that this time was different. From the corner of her eye, she saw Nelson reach for her serrated knife. He raised it towards her back, but before he could bring it down, she spun around with a piping hot dish of lasagna that she threw into his face. Nelson dropped the knife as he screamed in agony.

"I'm going to kill you!" He ranted as he squirmed around on the floor and she knew that he meant what he'd said. "You're as good as— "

The knife that plunged through his chest kept Nelson from finishing his threat. Instead, he began to gurgle and choke on the blood that bubbled up into his mouth. Robin cried out her apologies as she dialed 911.

Ten days later, Robin was cleared of any wrong doing. As the detective said, she had a right to defend herself. With pleasure, she threw dirt on Nelson's grave, inherited all of his money, and started life anew back in Houston, Texas with those that loved her.

Skeletons

Lawrence walked in the door and immediately felt uneasy. Something was off. He called Denise's name, but there was no answer. He put his keys down and started to walk through the apartment. It wasn't until he got to the bedroom that he saw the cause for the knot that had formed in his stomach. Clothes were strewn all over the room, costume jewelry was thrown about, and drawers were hanging out of the dresser.

"Oh no, please don't let her have found it!" Lawrence took off to the closet to look for the lock box he had hidden in the back behind some clothes. "Dammit!" He shouted as he threw the empty box across the room. He couldn't believe that she'd fell off again. He shook his head and realized that he could in fact believe it. As a matter of fact, he'd been trying to brace himself for the possibility of this happening.

Lawrence met Denise at a friend's birthday party three years ago. There was no denying that she was a gorgeous woman. Tall and statuesque with the body of a goddess. When she showed interest in him, his heart soared. They left the party together that night, went to a local diner, and talked until five a.m. Their connection grew from there and it wasn't long before he was totally in love with her. His friend had warned him to take things slow and to really get to know her.

"Man, Denise is a good girl, but she's definitely got a few skeletons in her closet. You know, habits that have haunted her for a few years," Daniel said as he gave Lawrence a serious look.

Lawrence had listened, but his feelings for Denise were all consuming. Within six months, he'd moved her into his apartment. For the first year, they lived like Cliff and Claire Huxtable, everything was beautiful. Then one day he came home to find Denise passed out with a tray of white powder and a straw on the coffee table in front of her. It didn't take a scientist to figure out that she'd been snorting cocaine. He was dumbfounded. He'd never heard her even elude to the idea of doing drugs. When she finally came to and sobered up, she admitted that drugs had been a big part of her past, but with intensive rehab, she'd overcome her addiction.

"If you overcame it, then why the hell were you in my apartment getting high?" Lawrence had demanded to know.

"Baby, I'm sorry. I ran into an old friend and he thought he was being nice by giving me a small bag of coke. I tried to push it away, but he insisted I take it. I planned to come home and flush it, but the temptation was too great."

With that confession, Lawrence suggested she go back to rehab. He'd never done drugs, but realized that her doing it this time was like opening Pandora's Box. Getting caught up in a life of drugs would be easier than ever now that she'd had another taste, but Denise refused.

"Babe, it was a one-time thing and in all honesty, I feel physically ill behind it. It doesn't have the effect it used to and feeling like this again is the last thing that I want. I don't need rehab, I just need you to trust me."

Lawrence took her for her word, but sure enough, he'd come home multiple times to find her high or getting high with some stranger in his place. This had been going on for the past two years. And here he was today with his place ransacked and the four-karat engagement ring he'd purchased for her a year ago was gone. He was hurt and angry. Angry that he hadn't locked the ring up somewhere outside of the house, but he just didn't think that her addiction would lead her to steal from him. Denise was no longer the woman he'd fallen in love with, no longer the woman he knew. He'd begged her multiple times to go to rehab, but she always refused. Now he was tired, tired of begging her to get clean, tired of finding strange folks laid up in his place high. He was tired of having his heart broken by her behavior.

Lawrence cleaned up his place, called a locksmith, and had the locks changed. He wept as he packed all of her belongings. He didn't know where she'd go, but he knew that she could no longer stay there. Early the next morning, he heard the door knob jiggling and the pounding on the door that followed.

He swung the door open and saw Denise standing there looking disheveled. "Baby, what's wrong with the door? My key didn't work."

"I changed the locks and I've packed your things, Denise. You're no longer welcome here. You've got to go."

Her eyes welled up and began to spill a fountain of tears. "Please Lawrence, give me one more chance. I promise I'll do better. I'll stop cold turkey. I swear I'll never touch that stuff again. I'll do anything to prove to you that I will do better. I love you baby. Please don't do this to us."

"Do you mean it; will you do anything to get better?" Lawrence asked.

"Yes, whatever you want," She assured him.

Within the hour, Lawrence was checking Denise into a sixty-day, intensive rehab facility. He kissed her on the forehead, told her that he loved her, and left her there to get clean and sober. He also took those sixty days to work on himself. He got back into church, started praying for God to order his steps, and he prayed hardest for Denise. He wanted to see her happy and healthy.

Two months later, Lawrence picked Denise up from rehab. She had returned to the beautiful woman that he knew her to be. They embraced for the longest time before he opened the door for her to slide into the car. She told him about her progress while he whipped through the city streets. It wasn't long before he pulled up to a beautiful apartment complex. He parked, opened her door, and escorted her to apartment 22L.

"Lawrence, this is lovely. A bit small for the two of us, but I guess we can make it work," Denise said as she looked around at the nice, but modest furnishings."

"It's not for us, Denise, it's just for you. All your things are in the bedroom, already put away neatly. I took the liberty of filling the refrigerator and the vanity with your personal hygiene items. I love you, Denise and I always will. I'll always be around to help if you should need me, but I can't do us anymore. It's not good for me and I don't believe that it's what's best for you. You need to stand on your own and create a good life for yourself."

Lawrence reached in his back pocket and pulled a check out of his wallet. "Your rent has been paid for the next six months and this is enough to tide you over until you start working again." He leaned in and kissed her on the forehead, turned, and walked away. Tears streamed down Denise's face, but she never tried to stop him. She knew that everything he'd said was right. It was time for her to grow up and be responsible for herself. She knew that he was tired of her foolishness and that they both deserved better.

Ghost in This House

Dara walked in the house after dropping her son off at school. She looked around in disgust. Her son's shoes littered the family room floor and school papers were strewn about the coffee table. The kitchen wasn't much better. Her husband, Rich, had left his dirty dinner plate in the sink, his glass on the table, and a laundry basket of clothes sitting on the floor. What annoyed Dara most was the fact that she cooked dinner the night before, cleaned the kitchen afterwards, and told her son, Bryson, to put all of his things away. She was annoyed that she'd spend her only week day off cleaning up behind the two men in her life.

The vegetables for dinner were all chopped, clothes all folded, shoes put away, and her house was clean again. Dara enjoyed the beauty of her home while she could because she knew that once everyone was back home, it would again look as if a tornado hit and she would be labeled the "nag" for complaining about them not putting their things away. That was something else she hated, how her husband and teenaged son teamed up against her, made her the butt of their jokes. They constantly called her OCD because she didn't like having things messy. When they weren't poking fun, asking for food, or where something was, they simply ignored her. Dara could feel herself getting emotional, but a glance at the clock reminded her that there was no time for that. She had to go pick her son up and get him to his internship. She turned on her invisible Uber sign and took off.

Later that evening, Dara returned home, cooked, and served dinner. She and Rich had agreed long ago that since she cooked, he'd clean the kitchen after dinner. Dara was lucky if he cleaned the kitchen once a week. Surprisingly, he took the initiative and started cleaning up. While he did the dishes, she went upstairs to shower and mentally prepare for the busy day to come. It wasn't long before Rich joined her in their bedroom.

"We gonna play tonight?" He asked as he started groping her body in a manner that he knew she hated.

"Rich, why would you do that when you know how much I hate it? That doesn't turn me on and doesn't make me want to be with you. Approach me with love and tenderness, not like some kind of pervert," Dara retorted.

"My bad, baby. You know I love you," Rich said as he groped her between her legs. "Don't give me a hard time, it's been a long day."

He ignored her protest, forced her back on the bed and did his business. No foreplay, no emotion, no love. The act itself lasted less than a minute and left her feeling as if he'd used her like he would a toilet. He did his business, rolled over and asked if she was going back downstairs because he wanted a bottle of water. Humiliated and angry, Dara went to the bathroom and took another shower to cleanse herself of all he'd left behind. She scrubbed herself and cried. This life was not what she had signed up for.

The next morning, Dara dropped her son off at school and headed to work. Because of Bryson's schedule, she'd had to cut her hours and go part time. Five hours later, she left work, rode across town to pick up her son, and then drove him back to the area she'd just left for his after-school intern program. It made no sense for her to drive home, so she went and enjoyed a late lunch at Panera. She ate her meal and reminded herself that once upon a time, she was completely in love with her husband. She focused on the fact that she'd begged God for a child and now it was her job to love and provide for him in spite of his smart mouth and failure to follow her rules and instructions. Left over love and responsibility is what was keeping her tied to her family. As she remembered how life used to be and realized what it had become, her eyes welled up and she couldn't stop the tears from making their journey down her cheek.

"Dara, is that you?" A squeaky voice called. "I haven't seen you in forever!"

Dara turned around to see her dear friend, Lena heading towards her. Dara grabbed a napkin and tried to dry her eyes before her friend reached the table, but she failed. Lena approached the table and held her arms out for a hug, but dropped them to her side when she saw that Dara had been crying. She promptly pulled out a chair and joined Dara at her table.

"Sweetie, it's great to see you, but not like this. What's going on?"

"Lena, I'm so sorry. I know you've called me a couple times and I haven't returned your calls. I haven't been a very good friend."

Lena waved her hand to dismiss what Dara was saying. "Girl, I'm not thinking about that. I know that life gets busy. Right now, my concern is you. What's going on? What has you in tears?"

Dara sat with Lena and spilled her heart. She told her old friend how she'd become a ghost in her own home. She explained that all her family wanted from her was what they could get from any maid. They wanted food, someone to clean up behind them, and to meet their arbitrary needs. Neither of them saw her for anything more than a servant. Then she clarified that Rich did see her as a periodic bed warmer, not a lover, not a friend, not a partner in life, just a bed warmer, a convenient place to put it. The woman she was and all that she'd accomplished in life disappeared when she walked in her home. Her family didn't see her, didn't even recognize all that she did for them. She was just a ghostly shadow, fading in and out of the background.

It broke Lena's heart to see her friend hurting. Tears stung her eyes as well and she knew that Dara had to change things.

"Sometimes we have to teach others and ourselves how we are to be treated. You know that I have room at my house and I'm inviting you to come and stay while you sort out what you want for yourself because this clearly isn't it. Time away will also give your family a chance to recognize you for the amazing woman that you are, not just their hand maid."

Dara didn't think twice. After getting her son home, she went and packed a couple of bags and left. She said nothing to her husband or son, but they both saw her heading for the door.

"Mama, I'm hungry. How long are you going to be gone and are you bringing dinner back with you?" Bryson asked.

"I don't know when or if I'll be back," Dara remarked as she continued her journey to the door.

"Humph, her little feelings must be hurt about something," Rich commented. "Come on son, we'll go out to dinner and let her get her priorities straight. But be warned, Dara, I'm not putting up with your little snotty temper tantrum for long. Get it together and be the wife and mother you're supposed to be."

"I love you guys. Bryson, I love you with all my heart and will continue to pray for you every day of my life. Be good and do your work."

Those were the last words Rich and Bryson heard from Dara for the next three months. The first two months were filled with reflection on all she'd sacrificed in the name of family. She tried to figure out when Rich had fallen out of love with her. More importantly, she realized that making her family happy shouldn't make her miserable. By the beginning of the third month, her decision was made, Dara would not return to their family home. When they'd leave for school and work, she'd return to the house to move more of her things out. Dara had returned to work full time and had even been given a promotion. She pulled half of she and Rich's savings and used it as a down payment on a condo. It was time for her to live a life where she felt valued and respected.

She finally shared her thoughts and plans with both her husband and son. She told them how they'd made her feel less than, how poorly they'd treated her, and how she could no longer accept that in her life. Bryson literally fell at her feet, rested his head in her lap, and tearfully apologized. Rich, on the other hand, shouted expletives at her back as she walked out of his life for good. Deciding to love herself more than the family picture they portrayed was initially a hard decision, but Rich's behavior made it much easier. Living a life where she was seen and appreciated trumped living as an unappreciated ghost every time.

Making Room For Better

Ember grabbed her bag and rushed from the office. It was her intention to leave ten minutes early, but just like every other day, she left ten minutes late instead. Mrs. Clora never gave her a hard time about her tardiness except for Wednesdays because that was the night of her Bible study class. Mrs. Clora had even told Ember that the next time she made her late for class, she'd have to not only drive her to church, but would have to sit through the class. The thought of participating in that class sent a chill down Ember's spine. She hadn't stepped foot in a church since her mother's funeral and had no intention of going back now.

Mrs. Clora opened the door before Ember could ring the doorbell.

"You're late, child and now you've made me late," Mrs. Clora scolded as she handed thirteen-month-old Lincoln over to her mom. "Let me grab my purse because you know you've got to take me to the church."

"Mrs. Clora, you've got to put Lincoln down more. She'll never walk if you keep carrying her around on your hip."

"I know you're not fussing at me! I've told you, when she's with me, she's mine and I'll treat her like I treated my own. Now get her in that car seat so we can go."

Ember giggled and kissed on her daughter while fastening her in her car seat. Lincoln jumped, kicked, and laughed along with her mom. She made all kinds of adorable noises as she attempted to communicate with Ember.

Ember ran around and jumped behind the wheel of the car as Mrs. Clora buckled herself in. Ember started the car, but before she could pull off, Justin pulled up and blocked the driveway.

"Where you going?" He yelled from his car window.

"I have to run Mrs. Clora to church. I'll be right back.," Ember shouted back with her voice full of annoyance. "Go on and park and let yourself in."

"Hurry up! I'm hungry and I ain't trying to wait on you all night," He barked as he backed up to clear the way for Ember to leave.

"I will never understand why you give that no good man the privileges that should be reserved for your husband. He's using you, girl. You know that you deserve better."

"You keep saying that, Mrs. Clora, but better hasn't knocked on my door yet."

"Child, you have to make room for better by getting rid of sorry as hell," Mrs. Clora replied with a twist of her neck. "Holding on to that no-good man is like asking God for a blessing but refusing to open your hand so that you'll have room to receive it. You have to make room for more, for better, child. But first you have to believe that you deserve more."

"Alright Mrs. Clora. Do you need me to come back and get you?"

"You could just get that baby and come in with me."

"You know that Justin is waiting for me at home," Ember replied.

Shaking her head, Mrs. Clora spoke softly, "One day I'm going to get you in there, but as for tonight, Ruby will drop me back at home."

Ember watched Mrs. Clora disappear through the church doors. She took a deep breath, looked back at her now sleeping baby, but stopped short of uttering a prayer. Instead, she headed home to Justin. Before she could get in the door good, he was all in her face.

"I told you earlier today that I was coming over. Why the hell isn't dinner ready? I mean damn, I could've gone home to my wife for this sorry ass treatment."

"Step back, Justin and give me a minute to put Lincoln down. I'll fix you some dinner, but I'm going to need for you to step back and chill. I can't take all your drama tonight."

"Oh, you can't take any drama. Bitch, all you are is drama. If you ain't asking me to leave my family, you asking me for money. You're the neediest bitch I've ever met. The least you can do is feed me at a decent time."

Justin's booming voice woke Lincoln from her slumber. She began to squirm and cry in her mother's arms.

"Great, you woke her up," Ember hissed as she moved around Justin. "Let me get her some milk and get her back to sleep."

"So, now you're putting her before me too?" Justin barked as he pushed Ember in the back, causing her to trip.

Stopping short of falling, Ember spun around with fire in her eyes. "If you make me fall and hurt my baby, I swear I'll—"

"You'll what, bitch? What are you gonna do to me?"

The more he screamed, the more he fussed, the more her baby cried, the more Ember replayed Mrs. Clora's words in her head. "You have to make room for better by getting rid of sorry as hell." Those words played over and over and again until Ember heard herself scream.

Justin was stunned by her outburst and even more stunned at what came next.

"If you can't call me by my name, you can't be here! If you can't talk to me with respect, you can't be here. If you can't be a better man, you can't be here!" Ember shouted.

She turned to go put Lincoln down and suddenly felt a sharp pain in the back of her leg. Justin had kicked her, causing her legs to buckle and down she and Lincoln went. Instinctively, she wrapped her body around her baby to shield her from Justin's blows. There was one kick after another until suddenly it was Justin screaming in pain.

Ember managed to sit up with the baby and was shocked to see Mrs. Clora and Ruby pummeling Justin with a bat and an umbrella. Ember had never seen anything like it in her life. She managed to get to her feet and ran to put Lincoln down in her crib and out of harm's way. She then dialed 911 before grabbing a knife and taking off towards Justin. Thankfully before she could reach him, Mrs. Clora stepped in front of her.

"Put it down right now! Ain't nobody going to prison over this piece of trash. You've got a baby to raise, now put it down!"

Angry tears strolled down Ember's face as she lowered the knife. Ruby was still holding a battered Justin with the point of her long umbrella pressed to his throat. By the time he managed to shove the umbrella away and run out the door, the cops had arrived and had him lying on the ground outside.

A week later, Ember was still thanking Mrs. Clora for all that she had done. Mrs. Clora had proven to be far more than a friendly neighbor. She was a dear friend, the mother figure that Ember had longed for since her mother's death. Mrs. Clora was heaven sent.

"If you want to thank me, come to Bible study with me. You and Lincoln come in with me tonight, there may be a word just for you, child."

Ember didn't speak, she simply parked the car. The three of them walked into the church and Ember couldn't help but notice the tears of joy that Mrs. Clora tried to hide. Ember couldn't deny that being in the church felt a lot like being home. Church wasn't a quick fix, but that night was the start of Ember's new relationship with God and a great source of strength. The lessons, the people, the love, it all taught her that she was worthy of better.

The weeks had turned to months and the months to years. Ember had stayed focused on building her relationship with God. She kept Him first and that helped her to be a better mother to Lincoln and place a higher value on her love. Many men had tried to talk to Ember, offered to take her out, but their offers came with conditions. Conditions that Ember was not willing to meet. She wanted to be an example for her daughter. She had to teach her daughter what was and was not acceptable for her life. But Ember couldn't deny that walking the straight and narrow could be a very lonely journey.

Ember pulled into the drive and went to Mrs. Clora's to pick up Lincoln. Mrs. Clora acted like keeping Lincoln for the past three years was no big deal, but both she and Ember knew better. The money Ember saved on childcare allowed her to stay in the quaint house she'd been renting since before Lincoln was born.

"Thank you so much, Mrs. Clora. I don't know what we'd do without you," Ember confessed as she took Lincoln by the hand.

"Child, I wish you'd stop thanking me every day. I know you're appreciative. Now do you mind if I ride to Bible study with you tonight?" Mrs. Clora asked.

"I'm so tired, Mrs. Clora. I was actually going to skip tonight."

"But the young associate pastor was going to teach tonight. You remember him? He's such a wonderful speaker and teacher."

"Mrs. Clora, I don't know who you're talking about. I don't remember ever hearing some young pastor, just the old heads that always teach," Ember moaned. She knew that Mrs. Clora was going to keep at her until she finally agreed to take her to church.

"Well he's a guest pastor, child and I really want to go. Ruby has to help her mother tonight and if you don't give me a ride then I'll have to miss it and I don't want to miss my blessing," Mrs. Clora rambled on.

"Okay Mrs. Clora, just give me a few minutes to get out of these heels and get a snack for me and Lincoln because I'm starving," Ember conceded before turning and heading towards her door.

An hour later, Ember unbuckled Lincoln from her booster seat while Mrs. Clora exited the front seat of the car. The threesome trotted into church and Ember prayed with every step that class would be super short tonight. They greeted everyone and eventually took their seats right up front where Mrs. Clora liked to sit. The pastor took the pulpit for a word of prayer before stepping down and taking a seat in front of the small gathering of congregants. Ember couldn't help but notice how attractive he was. She was sure she had never seen him before because he was too attractive to forget.

"Did I mention that he's single?" Mrs. Clora whispered as the pastor began to teach. "There's talk of him taking a permanent position in our church," She continued.

"Shhhh. Listen to the man, Mrs. Clora," Ember scolded.

"Don't shush me, child."

Thankfully, the pastor started to wrap class up a little earlier than usual. Ember was glad because she was exhausted, but a little disappointed because she was enjoying watching and listening to him. But class ended, and she grabbed her purse and was preparing to pick up a now sleeping Lincoln when Mrs. Clora interrupted her. When Ember turned around, she was face-to-face with the young pastor.

"Pastor Evans, this is my neighbor and friend, Ember. Ember, this is Pastor Craig Evans."

The two shook hands and exchanged pleasantries and Mrs. Clora tiptoed away and grabbed Lincoln. She left the couple to continue the conversation that they'd eased into. Fifteen minutes later, Ember found Mrs. Clora and Lincoln and headed home.

"So, what did y'all talk about?" Mrs. Clora inquired.

"Nothing much, just asked the basic get to know you type questions." As much as she didn't want to gush, she couldn't help herself. "And we exchanged numbers. He wants to go out to dinner," Ember confessed with a broad grin plastered across her face.

Ember parked in front of their homes and they all exited the car. Mrs. Clora started to walk towards her home when Ember stopped her.

"Mrs. Clora, I saw Ruby in class tonight. You didn't have to lie to get me to take you to church, but I'm glad you did."

"Baby, I may be a little older, but I'm still a woman and I know what it's like to be lonely. You're too beautiful and smart to be alone. Now that you've worked on yourself and grown in your walk with the Lord, you're ready for your better. Everything in me tells me that Pastor Evans is your better."

Two years later, Ember and Lincoln walked down the aisle and accepted Craig's hand in marriage. Mrs. Clora sat on the front row beaming with pride. She knew in her heart that this was going to be a lifetime marriage filled with mutual love and respect. She knew that this marriage would bear two more children and that eventually Craig and Ember would become the first family of the church. Mrs. Clora knew it all in her heart and she was right.

**Domestic violence is never okay. For help, please contact The National Domestic Violence Hotline @ 800-799-7233. **

A Mother's Love

Mama's Got A Man

Iris had put it off as long as she possibly could. Eight months ago, she'd finally agreed to go out with her co-worker, Lance. He was a tall, husky man, not her usual type, but handsome, kind, and respectful. That one date had turned into eight months of bliss. Iris was the happiest she'd been in a relationship since she'd first married her ex-husband. But she'd never allowed Lance to spend any time around the real love of her life, her daughter, April. Yes, he and April had met, but had only interacted for brief periods of time. April was well aware that her mama had a man, but she appreciated that her mom didn't allow her relationship to impede on the time that they shared.

That was then, but now Lance was ready to take their relationship to the next level. He had proven himself to be honorable. He had shown his love was true. With layoffs, Iris' job was being eliminated and Lance thought that this was the perfect opportunity for them to get married. Iris had to agree that it made perfect sense. Iris wouldn't have to pay the high rent on her condo, April wouldn't have to change school districts, and they loved each other. After sitting down with April and discussing the situation, expressing her love for Lance, and the benefits of their moving in with him while they planned a wedding, April smiled at her mom and gave her blessing. The twelve-year-old was not a selfish child and wanted to see her mother happy in all aspects of her life.

Moving day went off without a hitch. The transition was smooth, and April was happy that she got to stay at her school, maintain her friends, and even got a bigger bedroom. She and Lance have even bonded. He was a big jokester and she liked that about him. The only thing that didn't please her was how he loved to tickle her. That made her uncomfortable, but at the suggestion of her friend, she decided to not make a big deal of it. It was one little annoyance out of all the good.

"Now remember, April, I won't be home until late evening. Lance will cook you guys dinner. Please be responsible and do your homework, and I will see you by eight. Love you, sweetie."

"Love you too, Mom."

When April got in from school, Lance was in the kitchen putting the finishing touches on dinner. It wasn't long before they sat down to eat. Spaghetti was Lance's specialty and as usual, it was delicious. April got up from the table, did her daily chore of cleaning the kitchen, and then retired to her room for homework.

"Need any help?" Lance asked as he peered in April's door.

"No thanks, I'm almost finished."

April thought that her response would send Lance on his way, but he walked on into her room anyway. He stood over her shoulder and stroked her hair as she kept her eyes glued to her work. A few seconds later and his hand traveled from her hair to her shoulder, and then *accidentally* grazed her developing chest. April jumped from her seat and shot across the room. She grabbed her keychain and phone.

"If you move towards me, I'm going to call my mom and tell her what you did," April threatened.

Lance raised his hands as if to surrender and walked out of her room with a smirk on his face. "Please understand that your mom won't believe you and next time I won't just walk away," He assured her as he rounded the corner.

April sat and cried until her mom got home. She worried that her mom really wouldn't believe her, or worse, she'd choose Lance over her. When Iris finally made it home, her first stop was April's room.

"Hey baby girl, how was your day?"

April looked up at her mom with bloodshot eyes.

"What's wrong, April? Are you hurt, sick? What's the problem?"

Lance's words danced in her head, but April decided to tell her mom anyway. Before she could finish sharing the events of the day, Lance walked up and stood outside the door. But his presence didn't stop April from talking. Once she was finished, she looked at her mom and asked, "You believe me, right?"

Iris turned and looked at Lance, "Baby, is this true?"

"Of course not. We were joking. I tickled her and she took it the wrong way."

"Well I can't have my daughter going around shouting about my man being a molester. April, pack your things, it's time for you to go live with your dad."

"Mama, you don't believe me? How can you not believe me?" April cried.

"Pack your things, April. Pack them now!"

While April loaded her things in the car, Iris went into her bedroom to tell Lance goodbye. "Babe, I'm taking her to her father's house," She explained as she walked towards him. She leaned in to kiss him as she pulled her hand out of her purse. Distracted, Lance didn't see what she was holding. He didn't see her flip the switch, but he felt the electricity and the burning pulsing through his crotch. Lance fell to his knees screaming in agony, but it wasn't enough to make Iris pull the taser back.

"If you ever come near my child again, I promise I'll kill you." Finally, Iris pulled her weapon away. While Lance lay crying on the floor, Iris threw some things in an overnight bag and warned him to not be home when she returned for the rest of her things the next day.

"Mama, what was that screaming?"

"That was me saying goodbye to Lance."

Mute

Ben held his girls' hands tightly as they took the long walk down the aisle towards the coffin that held their mother's body. Angela, Ben's ex-wife had known for a while that she had an aggressive form of cancer, but chose to live instead of fighting with treatments that would make life not worth living at all. Angela unselfishly used holistic treatments to make her illness bearable while she taught her daughters, Shane and Elsie, all that she could about being proper, independent, educated young women. She took them to Bible study to help ensure they would have a relationship with God. Aside from their trust funds, she spent every dime she had to travel with them, exploring new lands and sharing adventures. If anyone could have squeezed a lifetime into two years, Angela proved that she was the one to do it. Lastly, she met with Gretchen, asked her to please love her babies as if they were her own and felt grateful when her ex-husband's new wife assured her that she would.

The day after Angela's service, Ben and Gretchen worked with the kids to pack up all of their belongings so that they could move into their new home. Ben was especially supportive and comforting. He'd always played an important and active role in the girls' lives. After he married Gretchen, she'd tried to get close to the girls, but couldn't deny that she'd found them annoying and needy. She felt that eight-year-old Shane was mouthy and five-year-old Elsie was a pathetic mute. The child only spoke when absolutely necessary and it was always in whispers. To her, Elsie was a brainless waste. Gretchen had every intention of letting the girls mourn for two more days, but Monday would be a new day and they would conform to her rules. If they refused, there would be consequences, very painful consequences.

Three weeks had passed since Shane and Elsie moved. With their father traveling four days a week for business, they were left alone with Gretchen more often than not. So far, they'd been sent to bed with nothing to eat at least three times and spanked almost daily for one infraction or another. Because of a promise they'd made to their mother to give Gretchen a fair chance, they hadn't said anything to their dad about her abusive behavior. But then Gretchen got angry with Elsie for spilling orange juice on her white pants.

"You ignorant little mute, look what you did," Gretchen screamed as she raised her hand to hit Elsie. When Elsie raised her teddy bear to block the hit, Gretchen tried to snatch the bear. Elsie screamed bloody murder and Shane quickly ran to her defense.

"My mom gave her that and you can't take it. Now leave her alone," Shane yelled as she wrapped her protective arms around her sister. That show of love enraged

Gretchen. She grabbed Shane by the hair and slammed her to the floor while Elsie stood crying with her bear covering her face.

To their surprise, Ben walked through the door. When he saw Shane on the floor, he dropped everything and rushed to swoop her up. "What happened here? Why is she on the floor and both of them crying?" When Gretchen didn't respond, he barked harshly, "Answer me, damn it!"

"They were running through the house playing when she tripped over Elsie and fell," Gretchen lied.

"No Daddy," Elsie said boldly, shocking everyone in the room. "She's did it, she hurt Shane. She hurts us a lot." Elsie then unzipped her bear and pulled out a small camera. Her mother had placed it there and told Elsie to press the bear's back whenever she was scared. She'd followed the instructions well.

When Ben hooked the little camera up to his laptop, he saw all of the evils that Gretchen had done to his girls. While Gretchen tried to explain, cry, and beg her way out of the situation, Ben dialed 911. They watched as the cops handcuffed and hauled a kicking, screaming mad woman out of the house.

When all the dust settled, Ben sat his girls down for a heart to heart. He apologized for not seeing past the facade that Gretchen presented. He wept with his daughters over the loss of their mother and for throwing them into an abusive situation. Finally, he shared with them the job offer he'd been presented with, one that would allow him to stay in town.

"Girls, I love you both so much and I swear that I will never put you in harm's way again."

Not Your Mama

Tori sat on her bed with her hands over her ears. Her mother, April was on the other side of the wall entertaining one of her many male guests. The banging of the headboard against the wall and the ridiculous moans were driving her crazy. Two minutes later, the noise stopped. Tori smirked and mumbled to herself, "Looks like you got yourself a minute man, April." It wasn't long before Tori heard the front door close and knew it was safe to emerge from her room. She slipped her feet in her house shoes and padded across the rickety floors until she reached the kitchen.

"Why aren't you asleep, Tori?" April asked in a harsh tone.

"Because I'm hungry. You made me go to my room as soon as your friend got here. Never mind that I hadn't eaten since leaving school. The least you could've done was brought me a sandwich in there before partaking of your activities," Tori sneered.

"Don't let that smart mouth of yours get you slapped," April barked as she pulled her ragged house coat closed. You sit there in judgement of me, but I'm doing this so that you can have food in here to eat and clothes on your back. So keep your judgements and try showing a little gratitude."

Tori knew that her mother was capable of far more than sleeping with men for money. She'd earned an Associate's degree in accounting when she was younger. She worked for a small company as their bookkeeper and was well respected by her coworkers. Then she met Randall, Tori's father. Within two months of meeting, April allowed him to move in with her. It was as if he'd cast a spell on her. It wasn't long before he had April doctoring the books at her job and bringing the company's profits home to him. As long as April did what he wanted, he was kind and gentle. But the days she showed up with empty hands and an empty purse, his love turned violent. That arrangement went on for only a month before April's employee caught on to her schemes. They'd compiled all of their evidence and had the cops waiting to arrest April when she reported for work. April received six months in jail for her crime and of course, Randall moved on to another woman while she was locked up. It was in jail that April discovered she was pregnant with Tori.

"Mama, I'm sorry for being flip with you, but it makes me sick to see you laying yourself down for these no-good men. You are better than this, you can do better than this!"

"Don't start that with me again, Tori. Some little two-bit job will not pay me what these dudes will. And remember, you are my child and if life gets too hard for you,

you'll do the same thing. You'll do whatever is necessary to survive. So, you can just get off of your high horse because baby, whoring is in our blood."

"Speak for yourself! I'm not nor will I ever be anyone's whore."

"Yeah, keep living girl. You're sixteen, built like a goddess and pretty. Any guy would be willing to pay good money for ten minutes with you. I can arrange it if you'd like and we can really use the money."

Tori left the food she was preparing right there on the counter and headed to her room. When she emerged ten minutes later, all of her belongings were stuffed into two white, drawstring trash bags.

"What are you doing?" April asked.

"I've called Auntie Liz to come pick me up. Mama, I can't stay here anymore. I'm your daughter, your only child, and you're willing to pimp me out for a few dollars? You need to understand that I am not like you and I never will be. I've got plans for my life and I won't allow you to derail them. I promise to check on you every week or so, but I cannot be here anymore."

Tori leaned in to kiss her mother on the cheek, but April slapped her face.

"You'll be back, you little ungrateful bitch," April sobbed. "Get out! Leave like your sorry daddy did. I don't need you anyway, I'm tired of taking care of you. Get out!" April slipped down to the floor in a puddle of tears, but her tears didn't stop Tori from walking out the door.

Just as she'd promised, Tori went to visit her mom every week. With her part time job at the mall, she was able to give her mom a few dollars here and there. That went on until Tori graduated high school and the local university. Despite April's refusal to attend either graduation or wish Tori well in her endeavors, she took every opportunity she could to brag to family and friends about her.

Years later, Tori went to visit a now old and frail April. Years of abusing her body had robbed her of her beauty. When Tori walked into the house, April immediately motioned for her to have a seat next to her. Tori placed the bags of groceries down and did as her mother wanted.

"Tori, I need to tell you how sorry I am. Baby, your father left me so hurt and so full of resentment that I withheld a lot of affection from you. I was unnecessarily mean to you and didn't treat you like a mother should treat her child. All of my hurt and anger for Randall I unfairly hurled at you. I've called you names that I regretted as soon as they crossed my lips. Now I need for you to know that you were right, you never were and hopefully will never be anything like me. Thank God, you are not your mama."

"Mama, everything about you isn't bad. You're intelligent and beautiful and I'd like to think that I got those things from you. I love you mama and I forgive you."

Two weeks later, Tori buried her mother. After the funeral, she began to clean out her mom's house and found a treasure trove of memorabilia all related to her. April had saved everything from Tori's first pair of baby shoes to the graduation picture she'd managed to steal from her sister. Tori cried as she poured through everything. She cried for the woman her mother should've been, the woman she settled for being, and the joy that had escaped her for the majority of her life. Then she cried tears of gratitude. She was grateful that she'd inherited only the best parts of her mother.

Love's Hard Lessons

Broken

CHAPTER ONE

Lauren had very mixed emotions about leaving Shady Hills. It had been her home for the past ten years. The doctors and nurses had served as not only her caretakers, but her surrogate parents after the unfortunate death of her mother and father. Initially she had fought everyone there and against every treatment they tried to provide. But after a few of the electro shock therapy treatments, she'd come to see that it was easier to be receptive to their methods than to have her head scrambled every couple of weeks. By the end of the first year, she had grown to love Nurse Rhonda and Doctor Albert, the other staff members she simply tolerated. All but Richard, she worshiped him, but after the incident she was no longer allowed to even entertain thoughts of him.

There was a soft tap on the door and Lauren turned to see Nurse Rhonda entering her room.

"I see you're just about finished packing. Did you double check your closet and dresser drawers to make sure you got everything?" Rhonda quizzed.

"Yes ma'am, I did like you said and put everything out on the bed so that I wouldn't forget anything."

"Your aunt should be here shortly. Has excitement finally started to set in for you? I know you initially wanted to strike out on your own, but I think staying with her for a while will serve you much better."

"I guess, Rhonda. It's not like I have much of a choice. The court mandate says that I have to be in the care of an adult until my twenty-first birthday. My aunt is nice enough, but I'd rather move in with you or simply move into my own apartment." Lauren looked at Rhonda as if she were hoping the woman would finally say "Sure, come on home with me."

"You know if they would have allowed it, I would've moved you in with me in a heartbeat. However, Dr. Albert has determined that an arrangement like that wouldn't be in your best interest. And the more I think about it, I have to agree with him. It's time you learn to stand on your own two pretty little feet. You have to learn to navigate life without being dependent on any of the hospital staff members." Rhonda explained. "But just think, you only have six months until your twenty-first birthday and then you can decide how you want to live your life without any interference from the courts or anyone else."

Lauren perked up at the thought of that. "You're absolutely right and I can't wait!" Lauren continued to pack the last of her things as she pondered her future. She'd already enrolled in a personal caretaker program. She was promised a job upon completion and was anxious to help others the way that Rhonda and the other staff member of Shady Hills had helped her.

"I did want to give you something." Rhonda said, snatching Lauren from her thoughts. "I got this for you, a while ago." Rhonda handed Lauren a white Pandora box.

"Are you sure this is for me?" Lauren asked with a childlike innocence.

"I'm positive. Now go on and open it," Rhonda instructed.

Lauren gently lifted the lid and pulled out a beautiful bracelet with two charms dangling from it. "It's beautiful," Lauren exclaimed as she marveled at the dove and the praying hands.

"The dove represents peace and freedom." Rhonda placed her hands lovingly on Lauren's shoulders. "You have both now and I want you to do everything in your power to protect them. The praying hands, well that's self-explanatory, but don't forget to always put God first. When you feel alone and don't know where to go or who to turn to, you can always turn to God. Talk to Him and he'll direct your path." Rhonda hugged her tightly. When she pulled away, she broke all the rules by sliding a folded piece of paper into Lauren's hand. She then blew her a kiss and left her to her packing.

Lauren wiped tears from her eyes and unfolded the paper. It was Rhonda's address and phone number with the message *if you ever need me, you'll know where to find me.*

CHAPTER TWO

Dr. Albert's secretary ushered Cloe Freeman, Lauren's aunt, into the doctor's office. "May I get you something to drink?" She offered. Cloe politely declined as she took a seat across the desk from Dr. Albert. The secretary took her exit, closing the door behind her.

Sensing Cloe's nervousness, Dr. Albert leaned on his desk and smiled warmly at her. "Relax, your niece has made more progress than any of us thought she was capable of. Lauren has grown into a bright, respectful young woman with goals for a productive future. I think you'll be pleasantly surprised with your new houseguest."

"I certainly hope so, Dr. Albert. I've been trying to be positive about everything, trying to calm my nerves. I'm not ashamed to admit that I'm still a little leery about having her in my house, but I know that it's what my sister would've wanted," Cloe confessed.

"Well I know that Lauren is grateful that you stepped up, making it possible for her to leave this facility and start her new life. She speaks kindly of you and how much you remind her of her mother. Allowing her to live with you, showing her that she is loved means a great deal to her. Now let's talk about her next steps. As you know, she's enrolled in a continuing education program where she'll earn a certificate as a personal caretaker. Have you made arrangements for her transportation to and from school?

"I have an old Toyota Corolla that runs like a fine oiled machine. I was going to give her some driving lessons, take her to get her license, and let her have that car. That way she'll have transportation when she's ready to strike out on her own. Plus, I figured she'd appreciate the independence of having her own car."

"That's very generous of you, Cloe. I'm sure she'll love having the car, but let's be careful not to toss her into the real world too fast. The point of her moving in with you is to give her a chance to ease into adulthood, to provide a smooth transition," Dr. Albert explained.

Lauren had finished packing and walked with her bags to Dr. Albert's office. His receptionist wasn't at her desk, so Lauren decided to let herself in. She stopped short when she heard a female voice.

"I understand that, Dr. Albert, and while I'm not going to toss Lauren to the wolves, I do plan to get her to a state of independence as soon as possible. Once she turns twenty-one, I want her to be fully capable of taking care of herself so that she can get her own place and I can get back to my life. I don't mean to sound cold and callus, but I chose not to have children for a reason. I simply do better on my own and I don't want another life dependent on me. I'm glad to help my niece, but let's be clear, this is a temporary thing."

Lauren shook her head in disgust and thought to herself, *Spiteful witch, I don't even want to go to your raggedy house. Believe me, my time there will be short and yours might be even shorter.* She tapped on the door twice and swung it open. The hateful glare she shot at her aunt did not go unnoticed by Dr. Albert and it sent a chill down Cloe's spine.

Trying to change the uncomfortable atmosphere that now enveloped the room, Cloe jumped to her feet and greeted Lauren with what was meant to be a warm embrace. However, it just made things more awkward than they already were. The tap on the back that Lauren gave in return was as cold as ice. Cloe was suddenly regretting everything that had seeped from her lips. She wondered if Lauren had heard everything or just her last statement. But it didn't really matter because she knew the last statement was the one responsible for the sudden chill in the air. She'd have to find a way to make up for it.

Dr. Albert moved from behind his desk, and placed his hands on Lauren's shoulders. "This is it, young lady, time for you to go conquer the world." At the site of tears dancing on the rim of Lauren's eyes, he pulled her into a warm, fatherly embrace. "You're going to be fine. I'll still see you at our weekly group meetings and you know that as long as there is breath in my body, I'll be here to support and guide

you. I'm only a phone call away."

CHAPTER THREE

Cloe helped Lauren lug her two bags into the house. "Let's leave the bags here while I show you around the house," Cloe almost sang. She was working overtime to try and be nice and make Lauren feel wanted. The expressionless face staring back at her let her know that her efforts were in vain. Still she persisted. "Follow me, it's nothing elaborate, but I love it."

"I don't need anything fancy and besides, I don't plan to be here but a hot minute anyway. You don't want me here and I don't want to be here, so let's not pretend otherwise," Lauren replied as she stayed two steps behind her aunt.

Cloe stopped in her tracks, took a deep breath, and turned to face Lauren. "Look, I'm sorry you heard the offensive part of what I said to Dr. Albert. Honestly, I wasn't trying to offend you or be mean, or talk badly behind your back. I was simply being honest. No, I don't want to be responsible for another human being for a prolonged period of time. I chose to not have kids for that very reason. However, I do love you and didn't hesitate to step up and offer to take you in. I do want to help you transition into a responsible, self-sufficient adult. If I'm wrong for any of that then too bad, it is what it is. Now, let me show you around."

Lauren was speechless. How could she be angry at someone who, for a change, wasn't tiptoeing around her and was so forthright and honest about her feelings? She didn't necessarily like her aunt, but had to respect her honesty. She followed her aunt from room-to-room, listened to her run down some basic house rules, and thought about how nice it would be if the house were hers and hers alone. After making their way back to the front door, Lauren grabbed her bags and drug them down the hall to her room.

Lauren put her things away and decided to start looking around on her own. She saw all the pictures of her mom that Cloe had placed throughout the house. Eventually, she made her way to the kitchen where Cloe was preparing lunch. "Can I help with anything?"

"No thanks, I'm just making sandwiches. Besides, you'll be responsible for dinner tonight," Cloe announced.

"You do know that I don't know how to cook, right?"

"Then it's time you learned," Cloe said matter-of-factly. "And I don't know if you heard or not, but I have a car for you and after lunch we'll go for our first driving lesson."

"You're giving me a car?"

"Yes I am. I know your impression of me is that I'm mean and don't want you around, but you need to understand that I love you and would never send you out into the world ill prepared to handle life."

~~~~

The first three months had flown by. Lauren had earned her certificate as a personal caretaker, become a licensed driver, and was interviewing for her first job. Things couldn't be better. Both Dr. Albert and Rhonda were incredibly proud of the progress she'd made since leaving the facility. Lauren had even made the decision to continue her education by enrolling in a nursing assistance program. While she and Cloe only seemed to tolerate each other, they'd found a way to coexist peacefully. She still maintained some level of respect for her aunt, but they simply didn't like each other. That aside, Lauren was pleased with her life and excited about her future.

She maneuvered her car through the city, careful to follow her phones GPS directions. This interview could change everything. It was with a family who was seeking a caretaker for their elderly mother. The pay was good, and this would position her to have enough money to move out on her own in three months. Lauren turned down a beautiful tree lined street and parked in front of a lovely French

Colonial home. After a couple of deep breaths to calm her nerves, a quick prayer as she fingered the praying hands charm that Rhonda had given her, she was ready to go get the job.

A slender, attractive woman greeted Lauren at the door. "Hello, I'm Lillian and you must be Lauren?"

"Yes I am. It's a pleasure to meet you."

"Please, come in. My mother is excited to meet you." The woman ushered her through the beautifully appointed house to the great room where her mother sat knitting. "Mother, this is Lauren Whitfield, she's here to interview for the position. Lauren, this is my mother, Ms. Alice Crane."

Lauren stepped to the chair where Ms. Crane was seated and extended her hand, "It is a pleasure to meet you ma'am."

"Likewise, please have a seat," Ms. Crane said as she gestured towards the armchair across from her. "So, dear, tell us a little bit about yourself."

Lauren proceeded to tell them about her certification and recent enrollment in the nursing assistance program. But to her dismay, Ms. Crane stopped her mid-sentence.

"Dear, we know all of that. The agency informed us of your education and qualifications. I want to know about your life, your family history, your aspirations for the future. I want to know about you and what makes you tick."

Momentarily thrown by Ms. Crane's request for personal information, Lauren cleared her throat and began to raddle off details of her life. She told the ladies that she was an only child whose parents died in a horrific house fire. Lauren told them about her Aunt Cloe who was kind enough to take her in and raise her as her own. She told them that she decided to go into this line of work to honor her parents whom she was unable to save. She expressed her desire to one day marry and have a big family. Lauren shared with them how lonely life had been without her parents or any siblings. By the time she was done, the ladies were damn near in tears. But she neglected to tell them that she started the fire that killed her parents. She failed to mention that she'd actually been raised in a mental institution. She never told them that her greatest desire right now was to have her aunt make a painful exit from this world. Lauren thought it best not to mention her fascination with fire and torture. Besides, she'd worked hard to put those thoughts of torture and death behind her, so there was really no point in telling them, right?

Needless to say, they offered her the job on the spot and Lauren gladly accepted. As she stood to leave, she noticed some of the pictures on the tables and hanging on the walls. For a minute, she thought that her eyes were deceiving her. Was that really Richard in the photos with Lillian? Couldn't be, but it absolutely was.

"What beautiful family photos. Is that your son, Ms. Crane?" Lauren asked.

Lillian laughed and answered for her mother. "Oh no, that's my husband, Richard. Dr. Richard May and he is the love of my life."

"Silly me, I should've known by the way you two are hugged up in the pictures. You make a lovely couple. Do you have any children?" Lauren tried to maintain a cool demeanor, but on the inside, she was screaming bloody murder.

"Not yet, but we're working on it," Lillian responded with a coy smile.

Lauren plastered a fake smile on her face. "Well good luck with that. I'm going to head out now, but I want to thank you both. Ms. Crane, I look forward to starting work bright and early Monday morning. I just know that we're going to have a wonderful working relationship."

"Yes, Dear, I'm looking forward to it. See you Monday."

Lauren was ushered back out of the house and wasted no time jumping in her car and speeding back out to the main road. As she drove, tears began to fall from her eyes. "I can't believe he's married. We loved each other, he should've waited for me," Lauren cried to herself. "But maybe this is the universe's way of telling me that I need to take him back. Yeah, that's it, this job is my sign to go after my man and take him back." Wiping her tears away, Lauren began to smile. "This is a gift, my reward for doing so well. Richard has been dropped back into my life and all I have to do is clear the path for us be together. Lillian is nice, but she has to go."

CHAPTER FOUR

Cloe was in the kitchen preparing dinner for her girl's night in. She was expecting four of her girlfriends to arrive with plenty of wine and lots to discuss. Hearing the front door slam, she called out, "Lauren, is that you?"

"Hey Cloe, it's me. What's going on, are you expecting company?" Lauren asked as she stepped into the kitchen.

"Yep, it's girl's night, remember? I was hoping that you'd decided to join me and my friends for dinner and drinks. We can celebrate your first week of work. I've cooked a little bit of everything and I think it'll be good for you to be social with other women."

"Is this part of your whole *turning me into a productive member of society before you kick me out* plan? If so, I think I'll pass. I actually have social plans of my own," Lauren said with a boastful smile.

"First of all, I was only trying to be nice and include you in on a fun night with the girls. So, your little smart comment wasn't necessary or warranted. Secondly, good for you, who are you going out with?"

"You're right, Cloe, I didn't have to get all snotty and for that I apologize."

"Apology accepted. Here, try one of these cheese puffs and tell me what you think." Cloe leaned across the granite countertop, extended a small platter of food. "I'm not sure if you'll remember them or not, but this is your mom's recipe. She used to make them all the time. She knew they were my favorite."

As Lauren bit into the cheese puff a smile played at the corners of her lips. The tasty treats brought back memories of her in the kitchen with her mom, cooking and laughing. Her mother was always a joy to be with. But the trip down memory lane quickly turned ugly as the warm memories of her mother were replaced with those of her perverted father, and how he'd take something as simple as eating a cheese ball and make it a nasty sexual act. She knew her mother loved her, but she failed to protect her from her father and that's why they both had to die. Cloe noticed how Lauren's smile turned into a scowl as she spat the cheese ball out into a napkin and threw it away.

"Do you think that there will ever come a time when you'll be able to separate the positive memories of your mom from the hurtful ones of your dad? She was a good woman and a good mother and deserves to be remembered as such."

Lauren looked at Cloe as if she had three heads. "She failed to protect me. What kind of mother allows a man to molest a child, let alone his own child? She stayed there while he had his way with me. She never said a word! What kind of woman would even marry a man like that?" Lauren screamed and cried her hurt and anger.

66

"I will not stand here and let you spew these lies anymore. It's time you know the truth about your mom and so-called daddy. That man who molested you was not your biological father! That punk ass man was sterile and couldn't have kids, but your mom was desperate for a baby and used a sperm donor. Ballard swore up and down that he was fine with her decision and vowed to love you like his own. But each month that you grew in your mother's womb, he grew angrier. He resented that he couldn't father a child and hated that some other man was responsible for you being created."

"You are lying!" Lauren screamed. "Why would you say that I came from a sperm donor? That's just spiteful."

"Think about it, Lauren. Why would I lie about something like that? You're too old to be this damn naive." Cloe moved around the counter, grabbed Lauren by the shoulders and shook her. "It's time for you to grow up and take responsibility for what you did. You killed my sister for no reason. I'm sorry that Ballard molested you, but your mother took an ass whipping every single day trying to stop him from hurting you. Every time he touched you, he had to beat her first. Your mother's body was covered in cuts, bruises, burn marks, all because she tried to protect you!"

Lauren sat stunned, mouth gapped open and tears pouring from her eyes. "I never saw her with bruises. She always looked perfect to me," She whimpered.

"How many times did you see her undressed?"

"Never, she never allowed me in her room or bathroom. She said it wasn't proper."

"You and I both walk around this house damn near naked all the time without a problem. She didn't let you see her because she didn't want you to see the scars. I've never been angry with you for wanting to kill that son-of-a-bitch, Ballard, but why did you have to kill my sister? Why did you kill Judith? She was the only family I had, and she loved you more than life itself."

"I'm so sorry. I didn't know, I swear I didn't know," Lauren cried hysterically.

Cloe wrapped her arms around her niece and held her tightly. They allowed their tears to cleanse them of the past as they hoped for a better future. They finally released one another, and Cloe returned to preparing the food for her girl's night. Lauren padded off to her room to prepare for her own evening. After a quick shower and makeup application, she draped herself in a sexy little sundress. Lauren emerged from her room refreshed and ready to go.

"You look great," Cloe complimented. "But you never said where you're going?"

"I promised Lillian that I would check in on Ms. Crane after hours. Lillian is out of town for the weekend and while her husband, Richard, is supposed to look in on Ms. Crane, I want to honor my promise and make sure that Ms. Crane is okay."

"You're dressed like that just to go check on your employer? I thought you said that you were doing something social?"

"Once Ms. Crane is settled, Richard and I may grab a bite to eat."

"Do you think that's wise? What if this Lillian chick doesn't want you being social with her husband? And what's her last name anyway?"

"Damn, you're so nosey, all up in my business. What Lillian doesn't know won't hurt her and if you must know, her last name is May. Goodbye!"

Cloe couldn't figure out why the name Richard May, sounded so familiar, but she hoped Lauren wasn't stepping into a dangerous situation.

CHAPTER FIVE

By the time Richard arrived at his mother-in-law's house, Lauren had already given Ms. Crane her dinner, a nice cup of hot tea, and put her to bed. Richard entered the house to find soft music playing and candles burning. To say he was confused would be a huge understatement. He looked around and stopped in his tracks when Lauren emerged from the shadows.

"Finally, we meet again," She said with a seductive smile on her face.

"Lauren, is that you? What are you doing here? I thought you were still at Shady Hills."

"Didn't your wife tell you that I was Ms. Crane's caretaker?"

"She told me that she'd hired a woman named Lauren, but I never imagined in a million years that it was you," He replied as he slowly walked further into the room. "I didn't think I'd ever see you again."

"I told you two years ago that we were destined to be together." Lauren threw her arms around Richard and breathed a deep sigh of relief when he returned her embrace. After a few moments, she pulled back so that they were face-to-face. She leaned in and kissed him passionately. Richard quickly came to his senses and pulled away.

"We can't do this, Lauren. I was wrong for getting involved with you at Shady Hills. You were a patient and I never should've crossed that line. Not to mention the fact that I'm married now, and I love my wife."

"You weren't wrong. What we had wasn't wrong, they just didn't understand."

Richard was a fresh-faced intern studying under Dr. Albert when they'd met. She was eighteen and he was twenty-six. Richard knew better than to become involved with a patient, but couldn't stay away from Lauren. When their affair was brought to light, he was immediately transferred, and she was never to speak of him again.

Undeterred by his protest, Lauren kissed him again, deeply and more passionately. "We can't do this," He whimpered. But Lauren persisted, she unbuckled his pants and set his throbbing manhood free. She dropped to her knees and took him into her mouth. Lauren stroked him, moving him in and out of her mouth until he thought he'd explode. Then she stood and allowed her dress to drop to the floor. He no longer had the strength to protest and made love to her right there on his mother-in-law's couch. He stroked and licked her like he used to, made her explode with complete satisfaction, and afterwards they laid there in each other's arms.

"We have to get up before Alice wakes and finds us," Richard stated as he began to reach for his clothes.

"We have all night. She was feeling restless and took one of her sleeping pills. She'll be out until morning."

"We still have to get up. This was wrong, Lauren and I never should've allowed it to happen. Lillian will be back in the morning and she's coming straight here. I can't do this to her. She's a good woman and doesn't deserve to be cheated on."

Lauren's demeanor completely changed, she became very hostile. "Am I not a good woman? Was I not good when I was on my knees? Was I not good three years ago when you were ramming your dick up my ass? You told me that you loved me and that one day we'd be together. Were you lying to me because you knew all along that I wasn't good enough?"

"That's not what I'm saying, Lauren. I did love you and I wanted to be with you, but that was years ago. Everything has changed. You're a good woman, but you're not and can never be my wife."

Richard bent down to retrieve his pants when Lauren grabbed a heavy, metal candlestick and cracked him over the head. He fell to his knees in agonizing pain.

"Please don't do this, Lauren," He begged as he tried to stand to his feet, but she hit him again, and again.

"I will not allow another man to use me and throw me away like yesterday's trash," She cried as she hit him again. "Not you, not my father," She sobbed as she hit him again. "I was going to kill her so that we could be together," She confessed. "I would've done anything for you!"

When she finally stopped swinging the candlestick, Richard lay dead on the floor in a pool of blood. "Oh God, what have I done?" Lauren shook her head, took some deep breathes, and decided her next move. She went to Ms. Crane's bedroom and retrieved the small handgun that she kept in the night table. It pleased Lauren that Ms. Crane didn't move a muscle. She really liked the old lady and didn't want her to suffer.

By the time Lauren returned home, every news channel was covering the story of the massive fire that had claimed two lives. Though the police hadn't released the names of the victims, interviews of the neighbors revealed that the home owner was Ms. Alice Crane. Cloe watched with her mouth gapped open. She knew that to be the name of Lauren's employer, and when Lauren walked through the door a bloody mess, Cloe's fears were confirmed. Cloe whispered to one of her friends to call the police and then instructed them all to hurry and leave.

With the house empty, Cloe began to question her niece. "What did you do, Lauren?"

"He wanted to use me and then throw me away, just like Daddy did," Lauren replied with an expressionless face. "I couldn't let him do that. I know the police will be coming for me, and I can't allow that to happen either," She explained as one tear rolled down her cheek. She pulled the gun from her pocket and Cloe was instantly gripped with fear. "Thank you, Cloe. Thank you for trying to help me, but I know now that I'm broken and beyond help. But I love you for trying."

Lauren lifted the gun towards Cloe and in one smooth motion, she turned it on herself and pulled the trigger. One shot to the head and Lauren fell dead on the floor.

In the following days, Lillian May learned about who Lauren really was and all that she had done. She also learned of her husband's past involvement with this mental patient. And just like Cloe, Lillian was left with no one. Everyone she loved was taken from her in one fatal swoop and life as she knew it would never be the same.

Where You Find It

Emory smoothed her hair with her perfectly manicured hands. She touched up her lipstick, gave herself a wink in the mirror, and mumbled "Let's go get our man." The bathroom attendant looked at her as if she were crazy, but Emory ignored the look and walked out full of determination.

She spotted Anthony at the table engaged in what looked like a deep conversation with Autumn. But Autumn was not her concern, her only care and complete focus was on winning the affection of Anthony. She approached the table and took the seat right between the two co-workers.

"So, what are we talking about," She rudely interrupted.

"Geez, do the words excuse me mean anything to you?" Autumn scolded.

"Sorry, I forgot how prim and proper you are. Always the lady," Emory replied sarcastically. "Please allow me to correct my ill-mannered behavior." Emory tossed her hair back, poked her ample breasts out and spoke in the most ridiculous, proper accent that she could muster. "Excuse me, loves, may I ask you to please recap the portion of the conversation that transpired in my absence?"

Anthony tried to hold his laughter, but failed miserably. Naturally, Emory shared in the laughter, she always laughed at her jokes harder and louder than anyone else. A slight nudge from Anthony broke Autumn's stern look and she too joined in on the laugh. Hers, as usual, was less authentic. She'd always found it hard to let loose in public and behave without regard to what others might think of her.

"Enough of this foolishness," Autumn chuckled. "We were just discussing the new temp employee in Anthony's department. She's done everything short of break her neck to get his attention. However, you know how he is, no mixing work with pleasure," She explained.

"If the right one would give me the time of day, I'd mix business and pleasure until you couldn't tell one from the other," Anthony responded.

Though his comment was intended to grab Autumn's attention, Emory snatched it as an opening for herself. "You know what they say, love is where you find it, even at the office. I have no issue dating someone that I work with," Emory commented while looking straight into Anthony's eyes and gently stroking his cheek.

Autumn couldn't deny that she was a little jealous of Emory and how strong she was coming on to Anthony. She'd never been able to work up the nerve to even wink at him, let alone serve herself up on a platter the way that Emory was doing. Instead, she lowered her head, allowing herself to become invisible while Emory flirted and carried on. But to her surprise, Anthony didn't flirt back with Emory. He didn't take her bait, but instead, he reached over and gently placed a finger under Autumn's chin and lifted her head so that they were the ones gazing into each other's eyes.

"Do you think that's true, Autumn? Is love where you find it, even if it's at work?" Anthony asked softly.

"I suppose it is true as long as people are willing to open their hearts to it."

"And my heart is wide open," Emory interjected as she shamelessly reached under the table and stroked Anthony's crotch. To her delight, he flinched, but didn't push her hand away.

When Autumn realized what was happening, she grabbed her purse and excused herself. They thought she was going to the restroom, but looking back at the table, she saw that Emory was now planting a kiss on his lips. Discouraged, she changed direction and headed out the door. She'd leave them to whatever it was they were about to do, and she'd spend another evening at home alone.

Anthony tried calling Autumn several times, but his calls went unanswered. After practically begging, Emory had convinced him to give her a ride home. She knew that once she had him alone, she could work her magic, spin her web, and he'd be hers for life. When they pulled up to her place, she acted as if she were so out of it that she couldn't possibly be trusted to make it to the door alone. Reluctantly, Anthony helped her get inside her place.

Playing along with her game, he asked, "Are you okay now?"

"I will be in just a few minutes," Emory teased as she threw her arms around his neck and started forcing her mouth onto his. "You know you're attracted to me and we both know that I can please you in every way imaginable." She whispered as she tried to pull him back into another kiss. But this time he grabbed her by the wrists and pushed her back, putting ample space between them.

"Do you know how easy it would be for me to screw you tonight? How I could take full advantage of you, having you doing things that a hooker on the street wouldn't even consent to? I'm trying so hard to respect you, Emory, but it's clear that you don't even respect yourself. I've watched you throw yourself at every decent looking guy in our office. When are you going to set some standards for yourself and stop thinking you can hook a man with good sex?"

His words stung like a swarm of bees, causing tears to well in the corners of her eyes. This was not the first time Emory had heard these words from a man, but it was her first time hearing them before the guy slept with her. "Forgive my behavior, Anthony. I didn't mean to make you feel uncomfortable and I certainly didn't want to come off like some desperate tramp," Emory sniffled. "I just wanted to feel loved."

"Why just feel love when you can be loved?" Anthony asked.

He turned her around and placed his hands on her shoulders. Anthony led her to the full-length mirror he'd spotted in the corner. "Remember, Emory, love is where you find it. I promise you that if you learn to love yourself first, others will have no choice but to love and respect you."

Anthony left her there with her thoughts while he went off in pursuit of Autumn. She was shocked to see that it was him banging on her door at 11:00 p.m.

"What are you doing here?" Autumn asked as she pulled her fluffy robe tightly around her waist.

"Autumn, Emory was right, love really is where you find it and every bone in my body is telling me that I'll find it with you. Please give us a chance?"

Autumn leaned in and gave him the sweetest, most tender kiss he'd ever had. She then leaned back and smiled, "Let's find it with each other."

Still Mad

Aubrey was tired. Tired of cooking, tired of cleaning, tired of supporting, tired of encouraging, just tired. She'd married Hurston twenty-two years ago. They'd met at work and the flirting started almost immediately. She was just flirting for fun, but he'd had a serious attraction to her. Over the course of six months, he'd managed to wear her down and she'd finally agreed to go out on an actual date with him. Two years after that date, they were married and within a year of marriage, the first of their four children was born.

At first Aubrey was pleased with their life. Both she and Hurston made a good living and enjoyed expensive meals out and fabulous trips. They laughed together, they were comfortable and satisfied in their space. But as the years rolled on, things began to change. She'd given up her career to raise her babies and that seemed to be Hurston's invitation to change the rules of the game. Aubrey was very limited as to what she could purchase for herself, but when it came to Hurston and the kids, the sky was the limit.

If all that weren't enough, Hurston had stopped making love to her and would instead use her body for his release once every three to four months. No romance, no foreplay, no kissing. Just him rolling over on her and rolling off satisfied sixty seconds later. It was humiliating. Aubrey had tried discussing her feelings with him, she explained that she had needs too. But Hurston didn't want to hear it. He reminded her that instead of worrying about her needs, she needed to be concerned with caring for her family. She needed to be there for him.

"I'm out here busting my butt to provide for this family and you want to talk about your needs? What about my needs? I need dinner on the table when I get home. I need to be able to talk about my worries and my concerns without being interrupted by your ridiculous demands for sex. Get your priorities in order, Aubrey!" Hurston barked.

Feeling dejected, Aubrey retreated to her bedroom where she could let her tears fall freely without harsh words from Hurston or questions from her children. Sniffing and wiping tears, she hadn't noticed her youngest ease into the room.

"Mom, may I ask you a question?" Evan asked, but didn't bother waiting for an answer. "Why are you still with Dad?"

"Because we're a family, you guys deserve to be raised in a two-parent home. There's nothing your dad won't do for you all. If we weren't married, I couldn't guarantee that he'd still be the provider that he is right now," Aubrey explained.

By this time, her other three kids had joined them. They encircled her, tried to comfort her, but Aubrey was ill prepared for what came next.

"I'm sorry, Mom, but Dad is seeing another woman," Nelson, her oldest blurted out. He introduced us to her when he took us out to Dave & Busters last weekend. They acted like it was a coincidence that they were both there. He introduced her as his coworker, but later when I went to the restroom, I spotted them in a corner kissing. You deserve better, Mom."

When Hurston returned home, she confronted him about his affair. She never said how she'd found out and he never denied it. He explained that after four kids and no job, she'd lost her appeal.

"No offense, but your body isn't tight like it used to be. You don't dress nice for me the way you used to, and you never seem to be into the sex when we do indulge. The package that used to turn me on now does nothing but turn me off. You let yourself go, Aubrey."

"My body changed because I birthed your four children. I don't dress up because you don't allow me access to our money."

"You mean my money," Hurston blurted.

In that moment, Aubrey decided to show him who's money it really was. Nine months later, a judge awarded Aubrey the house, $6,500 a month in child support, and half of Hurston's 401K which was a decent $230,000. To say that Hurston was pissed was a major understatement, but there was nothing he could do about it.

Four years after their divorce, their youngest child was preparing to leave for college, Aubrey had re-entered the work force, she was dating a gentleman that was eight years her junior, and Hurston was still mad.

The One Who Loves You

Reesie stood to her feet and faced her newly declared ex-husband. "I'm sorry that this is the end of us. I never meant to hurt you. I still love you, but after all that I've done and regardless of what you say, you'll never be able to truly forgive me."

"Please don't blame your decision to leave on me. I told you that I forgive you, but I understand that with me is not where you want to be. And as much as it hurts, I love you enough to let go. I just hope that he loves you the way that you deserve to be loved," Carlos said as he caressed her hand before gently letting it go.

Reesie thanked her attorney, turned and left the building. She rode through the city reflecting on the events that led to today's signing of divorce papers. She and Carlos had met eight years ago. Her initial thought was that he was not her type. She was attracted to tall, dark, physically fit, and incredibly handsome men. All her friends teased her about being a magnet for pretty boys. Carlos was not a pretty boy. He was cute, but his five-foot ten-inch frame carried more weight than it should. He wasn't obese by any stretch of the imagination, just a little too puffy for her liking.

But he was a charmer with a heart of gold. He'd come into her bank requesting help with his business accounts and by the time he left, he had Reesie's number. She'd reluctantly agreed to go out with him and a year later, she agreed to be his wife.

Their lives had been beautiful, filled with love and laughter, but still something was missing for her. Reesie missed the passion. The wild love making that made her body explode time and time again. Sure, Carlos was a decent lover, but she wanted that wild passion of days gone by. Imagine her surprise when her ex-lover, Tony, tracked her down. Against her better judgement, Reesie agreed to meet him for lunch one day. That lunch date turned into an all-out affair. She snuck around behind Carlos's back for six months, lying and sleeping with Tony. She felt an enormous amount of guilt, but what Tony did to her body out weighted the guilt. Then Tony confessed his love and begged her to leave her husband. He wanted her to be available to him all the time. He no longer wanted to share her with anyone. Foolishly, she agreed and now her marriage was officially over.

Reesie walked into the hotel room to find what seemed like a million candles sparkling. Tony had champagne on ice, roses everywhere, and his arms open as soon as she crossed the threshold. "Is it done, are you free?" He asked.

"I'm all yours, baby." Reesie ran to him and they embraced the way that lovers do. "We can build the life we've always wanted, Tony."

"Yes, yes we can. I say we toast to this momentous occasion with a little champagne." Tony grabbed two glasses, filled one and began to fill the other when Reesie stopped him. "What's wrong, baby?"

"Nothing, nothing at all, but I'd prefer to toast with water," She said with a broad smile.

"Why?"

"Tony, we truly get to be a family. Baby, I'm pregnant."

"You're what!" Tony barked

"I'm pregnant, just like we talked about, remember? You said you wanted us to build a family."

"Why the hell did you have to go and ruin everything! You're so stupid. I already have a family, Reesie. A wife and three kids waiting on me every night. How the hell am I supposed to afford another kid?"

"What do you mean you're married?! You just had me divorce my husband for you. You said you didn't want to share me."

"And I don't, but I don't want this either. I love you, but I can't deal with another kid. Hell, I don't even trust that it's my kid. I'm sorry, but this is not what I signed up for. Let me know when the baby is born and I'll show up for the paternity test. Until then, lose my number," Tony said as he grabbed his things and left.

Eight months later, Reesie found herself living back home with her mother and a new baby. She thought her mom would berate her every chance she got, but all her mom said was "I told you, if you ever had to choose between the one you love and the one who loves you, always pick the one who loves you. You chose wrong, baby."

Guilty Before the Sin

Addison looked at her husband with loving eyes. She admired his slim but strong physique. The way Danny's skin glistened as he stepped out of the shower was such a turn on. Addison's mom had always told her that as long as a couple loved the way each other looked naked, then their marriage was on solid ground. If that statement were true, then surely, she and Danny would be married forever. Their bodies weren't perfect, but they were perfectly made for each other.

Danny finished drying off and sauntered from the bath into the bedroom where Addison lay across the bed watching him like a hungry lioness. He reached the bed and leaned down to kiss his wife when Addison bounced to her knees and abruptly shoved him away.

"What the hell is that, Danny? Who's been kissing on you and leaving passion marks? I can't believe you're cheating on me and damn it, you're too old for this foolishness. How could you?" Addison screamed with fire in her eyes.

"Here we go," Danny said as he turned and headed towards the chest of drawers. "I'm going to tell you this one more time, I have not, nor do I plan to ever cheat on you. No one has been kissing on me and passion marks are for teenagers."

Danny slammed the drawer closed and pulled on a pair of pajama pants. That was a true sign to Addison that no intimacy would be happening tonight.

"Well, what am I supposed to think, baby? You've got three different red marks on your chest and one on your neck. They didn't just appear out of nowhere! I'm trying to understand how you can claim to love me, but walk around with evidence of your infidelity all over you."

Danny walked back over to Addison and yanked his t-shirt back off. "Do you still see the marks?"

Addison inspected his chest, but only saw the remanence of one mark. "What did you do, where did they go?"

"Use your common sense, Addison. I'm light, bright, damn near white and bruise easily. Those marks came from my drying off. And please understand that I'm getting real sick of this crap. Stop always expecting me to do you wrong. Stop looking for stuff that just isn't there." Danny pulled his shirt back on and headed out of the room.

"I'm sorry, baby. Please come to bed," Addison pleaded.

"I am going to bed, in the guest room." Danny stormed off, completely disgusted by his wife and all of her insecurities.

The next morning, Addison got up and made a lovely breakfast for Danny before leaving for work. When he emerged from the guest room, Danny found pancakes, bacon, fresh berries, coffee, and a note of apology. He was in the middle of his meal when the doorbell rang. Shirtless, he glided to the door to see who had darkened his doorstep. To his surprise, Emily, Addison's best friend, was standing there with a smile plastered on her face.

"Hey Em, what are you doing here?" Danny asked as he welcomed her in.

"Addison was supposed to have left a box of books for me. My sorority is doing a book drive today and I told her I'd swoop by and pick up her donation."

"Oh, that must be the box in the corner of the kitchen. Come on in for a minute, I'll throw on a shirt and take it out to the car for you. It's some more coffee in the pot, pour yourself a cup," Danny offered.

"I think I will," Emily remarked as she grabbed a cup and poured a cup of Columbian roast.

Danny emerged from the back of the house about three minutes later and sat down to finish his meal while Emily sipped on her coffee. They shared small talk before Emily asked a question that caught Danny off guard.

"So, you guys are almost a year into the marriage. How is it going, I mean the whole insecurity thing?"

Danny almost dropped his fork. "Did you know about Addison's insecurities before we married?"

"A lot of us did," Emily confessed. "We assumed you did as well."

"I had no idea. She did not display this foolery before we married, but now I always seem to be guilty even though I've committed no sin. I'm so tired of having to account for every minute of my day, explain every mark that may show up on my body, and reassure her that she's just as beautiful as every other woman. Its damn exhausting."

Emily rose from her chair and moved closer to Danny. She placed her hands on his shoulders and started rubbing gently. "I hate to tell you, Danny, but it's not going to get any better. She'll keep accusing you until you actually cheat. I mean, if she's accusing you, you may as well have all the fun she thinks you're having."

Danny slid from under Emily's grip and moved to the other side of the kitchen island. "You know, when I married Addison, I did so with the intensions of being faithful. I love Addison and while her constant suspicions are annoying, they're not enough to make me actually stray."

"Are you sure?" Emily asked as she approached him again, seductively placing her hands on his chest.

"I'm positive, Emily. Now let's get this box to your car," Danny said as he pushed her away, grabbed the box, and walked it out to her car.

Later that evening, Danny came home from running errands. He was ready to forgive his wife and spend the evening making love to her. As he walked through the house looking for his bride, he heard what sounded like he and Emily's conversation from earlier. He followed the sound and found Addison watching a recording of his interactions with Emily earlier that day.

"What the hell is going on? Addison, did you record me today?"

"I did and I'm so proud of you! I feel blessed to be married to such a faithful man," She said as she threw her arms around his neck. "Do you know how many guys have fallen for that? But not you, babe. You love me, you really love me."

"Yes, I do. Too bad we can't stay together. Your insecurities and accusations are way more than I can handle. This is sick, and you need help. No one should doubt themselves, their marriage, or their spouse this much. I love you, babe but I can't, I won't live like this.

Within thirty minutes, Danny had packed some of his belongings and left his bride in a puddle of tears. He didn't see her again until they stood before the judge that finalized their divorce.

Just As I Am

The coffee shop was packed, so what were the chances of Carma bumping into her old love, Clifton? But just as sure as it was Monday morning, there he was standing right in front of her, flashing that brilliant smile.

"Carma, is that you? Wow, how long has it been? You look amazing!" He exclaimed as he wrapped her up in a strong embrace.

For Carma, it was as if everyone disappeared and only the two of them were left. She inhaled his scent and melted in his arms. She finally snapped out of her trance as he started to pull away from their embrace. Finally finding her voice, she asked "What are you doing in the city? I thought you moved back home to Manassas to help your parents with their business."

"I did, but they decided to sell the business and retire to Florida. I figured this was the perfect time to come back to Atlanta and you know, pick up where I left off." He explained as he stroked her short curly hair.

Carma tried to make herself remember how hurt she was when Clifton left her for another woman. Tried to remember the feeling of humiliation when he told her that thick thighs were sexy, but her fat ones were not. She fought to remember the feeling of inferiority that smothered her when he took her on a surprise date with his ex-girlfriend and told her that with a little liposuction she too could be that fine. As he droned on about how he'd landed a great position and had purchased a new condo, Carma begged herself not to be so mesmerized by his fine body and memories of how he made her feel when they made love.

"Did you hear me, baby girl?" He asked as he snapped his fingers a little too close to her face. "Where did you go just then? It was like you checked out on me. Anyway, I was saying how good you look. I love the haircut and clearly, you've been working out."

"Oh, well thank you. I figured it was time I took better care of myself. I must admit, I feel stronger and lighter. Not just physically, but emotionally as well. I'm in a really good place."

Clifton reached for her hand and asked her to join him at a small corner table. Ignoring the time, she followed him like a little puppy dog. Just like she used to before he broke her heart. They shared light conversation, reminisced about old times, and old friends. He stroked her hand and spoke of how beautiful she looked. Then he said something that made all the feelings she couldn't seem to find earlier come crashing through her heart.

"You look amazing, but the weight loss deflated those ample boobs you had. Have you thought about breast augmentation? And please don't take this the wrong way, I love your haircut, but a long weave cascading over those sexy shoulders would look amazing."

"You think so?" Carma asked nonchalantly.

"Yes, I do." Clifton checked his watch, "Carma, can we continue this over dinner tonight? I'd love to reconnect, really spend some time together."

"That sounds great. Where would you like to meet?"

With a sly grin on his face, Clifton asked, "Do you still live in the same house?"

"Of course, I do. I love my house," Carma smiled sweetly.

"How about I come over at eight this evening?"

"Sounds good, I'll see you then," Carma blushed.

"And wear something sexy," Clifton said with a wink before taking his exit.

Eight o'clock found Clifton standing on Carma's front porch ringing the doorbell. He was feeling especially lucky and just knew that they would end the night with a hot romp in the sack. After all, despite her flaws, Carma was great in bed. The door swung open and he was pleased to see her dressed in a slinky, sexy dress and heels.

"Come in Clifton. We've got an amazing meal waiting."

Clifton followed Carma to her candle lit dining room. The food smelled amazing and he was ready to enjoy *everything*.

"Take a seat, Clifton and I'll be right back." Carma turned and headed to the kitchen. When she returned, she was followed by a tall, chiseled, handsome man who carried dishes filled with scrumptious food.

"Wow, you hired a chef to serve us?"

"Not exactly, Clifton. This is my husband, Tyson. You see, he respects me, he pampers me, he loves me, and makes love to me better than anyone ever has. Unlike you, he's never tried to make me over, he accepts me just as I am."

Clearly annoyed, Clifton stood to his feet and asked, "If he's so great why did you bother inviting me over?"

Tyson stepped to Clifton and with a smile on his face, he responded, "She wanted to give me the pleasure of telling you what a fool you are. And now I get to toss you out. This dinner is for me and my baby, so if you'll excuse us, we've got food to eat and love to make."

Clifton was soaked in humiliation. As he shuffled to his car, he asked himself, "Damn, is this how I made her feel all those years ago?"

He Never Left

Bella fell to her knees, shocking even herself, and began to beg Tylen not to leave. She wrapped her arms around his legs as he tried to empty his dresser drawer into a tote bag.

"Tylen, baby please. You can't just throw away fifteen years. You have to remember that we love each other. We've loved each other for half our lives. There is nothing out there that can touch what we have here in our home. Baby please!"

Annoyed, Tylen reached down, grabbed Bella by the arms and threw her back to the floor. "Where is your pride? Look at you, you're an attorney groveling on the floor like some starved dog begging for bones. This right here is part of the reason I'm leaving.

"What reasons could I have possibly given you to treat me like this? I've done my best to be all that you could ever want in a wife. I cooked for you, cleaned up behind you, hell I've even bathed you. What else could you possibly want?" Bella sobbed.

Tylen looked down at his beautiful wife and wondered where was the woman he first fell in love with. She'd turned from the strong, smart mouthed, down for the cause girl she was when they met into some Stepford wife clone of her mother. In his eyes, the only thing she had going for herself was her thriving law practice.

"Get up off the floor!" He demanded. "Bella, it was never my intention to hurt you. I've tried to tell you how much I miss the woman you were during our early years. You were passionate about life, you enjoyed living on the edge, and being spontaneous. That's who I married and now, that's what I'm missing."

Bella plopped onto the edge of the bed. "Tylen, I'm still that woman. Baby I'm still spontaneous and passionate."

Tylen dropped everything in his hands and rushed over to Bella. He lifted her to her feet, began to kiss and undress her. When she tried to pull away, he pulled her closer and started stroking her body. But when he tried to unbutton her pants, she more forcefully pulled away.

"Give me a few minutes, Tylen. I just need to freshen up."

"I want you just like you are. I want you now," Tylen said.

"I just need ten minutes, babe."

"And I need to go." Tylen gathered his bags and walked out, leaving Bella drowning in a pool of her own tears.

Three hours later, Bella's mom found her still crying in the middle of her bed. "Bella, I want you to get up and go wash your face."

"Mom, I don't want…"

"I didn't ask you what you wanted," Martha interrupted. "I told you to go wash your face and then I want you to meet me in the kitchen. Now go."

Martha waited patiently for her daughter to join her. When Bella finally settled in a seat at the table, her mom took her by the hands and asked, "Why are you crying over this man?"

"Mama, you know why. He left me, and it feels like my heart up and walked out of my chest. He was my everything. All I tried to do was put him first and love him the way that you've done with Daddy. Instead, all I got was left. The one who was supposed to be my everything left me."

"Baby girl, you clearly weren't trying to be like me. I love your father and will until the day I die, but he is not first in my life and he has never been my everything. God is my everything and He is who I put first. You are losing your marriage because you put that average man above our supernatural God. Instead of humbling yourself before God and asking for His direction with your marriage, you humbled yourself before Tylen. And yes, he has left you, but the one that matters most has never left. Martha pointed upwards and said, "He never left. And now I suggest that you bow your head, humble yourself, and ask his forgiveness. He is a jealous God and will remove whatever you put above Him. But whatever He takes, He can restore. Go

before the throne, baby, and get your head and heart in order."

The Best Thing About Love Is Us

Right Under Her Nose

Christie sat on the bed with her knees drawn up to her chest, rocking back and forth like a troubled mental patient. Tears streamed down her face. Her eyes so swollen from crying that she looked as if she'd just gone ten rounds with Floyd Mayweather. The drama that came with trying to keep her relationship with Jerrod afloat was becoming too much to bear.

The doorbell rang, but Christie chose to stay where she was, in the traumatized state that she was. Although she didn't want to move, the persistence of the person at her door forced her to get up. The incessant ringing was going to drive her crazy otherwise. "I'm coming," She shouted in a gravelly voice. Christie swung the door open and burst into tears all over again.

In one swift move, Winston stepped inside, closed the door, and took Christie in his arms. He could feel how weak she was physically and emotionally, and it broke his heart. He swooped her up and carried her to the couch. He sat down, holding her in his lap as if she were a toddler. "What happened over here, Christie? What has Jerrod done now?"

"Why do you automatically assume it was him?" She whimpered.

"Because it's always him," Winston said very matter-of-factly. "Now, what happened?"

"I have to say that things probably wouldn't have gotten so out of hand had I not been questioning him like he was on trial for murder. He had a job interview this morning with an accounting firm. It seemed like a very promising opportunity, but when he returned an hour later, he was all pissed. Instead of letting him cool down and decompress, I asked him how it went," Christie explained as tears ran from her eyes like water from a fountain. "He said that they wanted to bring him in at the entry level with an entry level salary. Still, I pushed by saying that I didn't see anything wrong with that and that he should've jumped at the opportunity and that's when all hell broke loose."

"Did he put his hands on you, Christie? Did he hit you?" Winston demanded.

"No, he just grabbed me and pushed me against the wall. He said that my statement was disrespectful and showed just how little I thought he was capable of. When I explained that he could use this position as a stepping stone, he raised his fist and smashed it into the wall right by my head. I thought he was going to knock me out," She said as she buried her face in Winston's chest.

Winston's jaw tightened as he lifted Christie and sat her on the couch. He walked to the kitchen to retrieve a glass of water for her. As he walked back to the family room, he saw the indention in the wall. "I hope the bastard broke his hand," He mumbled.

"What did you say?"

"I said I hope the bastard broke his hand!" Winston huffed. "Christie, I don't understand why you continue to stay with him, why are you so tolerant of Jerrod? You are a beautiful, brilliant, successful woman that any man would feel blessed to have. Yet you keep this jackass around and subject yourself to his abuse."

"Didn't you hear me when I told you how I questioned him, how I doubted him?"

"I heard you sounding like a victim of domestic violence, that's what I heard."

"Jerrod has never hit me, and I don't appreciate you comparing me to some weak, abused girlfriend," Christie shouted.

"Educate yourself, Christie. Victims of domestic violence aren't weak, they've been abused either physically, emotionally, financially, or all of the above. He doesn't have to hit you to abuse you. Meanwhile, you've got real love right under your nose, patiently waiting for you to realize your worth and get rid of that loser."

Before Christie could reply, the door swung open and there stood Jerrod, bat in hand and ready to go to war."

"What the hell is he doing here?" Jerrod barked

Christie jumped to her feet and ran to get between the two men. "Baby, he just came by to check on me, wanted to make sure that I was okay."

"Why the hell wouldn't you be okay?"

"Because you're up in here slamming her against walls instead of taking responsibility and accepting whatever job you can get," Winston said with fire in his eyes.

Jerrod raised his bat and lunged towards Winston, but when Christie tried to push him back, he grabbed her by the hair and flung her down. Winston tried to catch her, but she went down too fast and her head slammed into the metal umbrella stand. Blood oozed from the gash on her forehead as she lay unconscious. Like the coward he was, Jerrod dropped the bat and took off running while Winston dialed 911.

Three days later, Christie was released from the hospital and Winston was right there to take her home. As they drove the city streets, she caught him stealing glances at her. She uncourteously touched the bandage that covered the stitched gash on her head.

"You are so beautiful," Winston said with a smile.

"Did you mean what you were saying before Jerrod burst into the house, you know about love being under my nose?" She asked sheepishly.

"I absolutely did. It's my greatest desire to show you just how serious I am."

After a year of counseling and self-discovery, Christie stood before Winston in a beautiful garden dressed in a white, silk jumpsuit. He was in a casual white suite and they were surrounded by their closest friends and family. This was a marriage orchestrated by the angels and blessed by God Himself.

The Red Room

Nelson stood back and watched his wife as she draped her body in a sexy sheath dress. The six-inch heels that she wore made her calf muscles pop and her long legs look even more appealing. He tried not to get jealous when she dressed like this to go out with her girls, but couldn't help but wonder why she didn't dress like that when they went out together. He'd asked her a few times, but the answer was always the same, "It's not appropriate for the places you like to go." But he didn't see what was wrong with dressing like that to go everywhere.

Trinity grabbed her purse, gently kissed Nelson on the lips, and told him that she'd be back in a little while. He told her that he'd be waiting up and watched her saunter away. Normally, Nelson would wait at home like the devoted husband he was. He'd watch television, maybe drink a beer, take a nap, and hope that she'd feel like having sex when she returned.

When they first married, Trinity wanted to have sex all the time and she wanted it everywhere, the bed, the kitchen, the balcony, but Nelson was a creature of habit.

With him, sex was reserved for the bed, him on top, missionary position. It didn't take Trinity long to tire of that routine and start denying Nelson sex altogether. She'd told him that if she couldn't be sexually satisfied, neither could he.

Out of frustration, Nelson decided to change things up tonight. He grabbed his keys and headed out the door to a place he swore he'd never go, the strip club. Twenty minutes later, he was parked outside of the Red Room. He'd been taught by his devoutly religious family that such places were the devil's workshop, but something had to give, and he figured watching without touching couldn't be that big of a sin.

He entered the nicely appointed club, surprised that it wasn't the seedy, grimly looking atmosphere that's always depicted on television. Instead, it was an upscale club with gorgeous women of every nationality dancing and trying to entice the big spenders that flaunted their money. Nelson was only halfway through the club when he spotted a table full of beautiful women, one of them being his wife. Instead of approaching, he decided to sit at a corner table and observe. He was completely shocked when a call went out for all amateur dancers to take the stage and his wife sprang out of her seat. She and three other women would dance for the title of Red Room Seductress.

It took everything in Nelson not to rush the stage and yank Trinity off. But instead, he sat there and watched her slowly twirl around the pole. He raised a brow when she dropped her dress to the floor and enticed the crowd with her tight body. The pink lace bra and thong left very little to the imagination. Watching her ride the pole like a pro had his manhood throbbing.

"Excuse me, Miss. Is it possible to get her alone?" He asked one of the waitresses.

"For a few hundred dollars, I can escort you to one of our private red rooms. If she's interested, she'll join you shortly. If she's not, you can pick another girl."

Nelson paid the fee and waited inside the plush room. Part of him wanted her to hurry and walk through the door, while another part ached for her to turn the offer down. Five minutes later, the door opened and in walked Trinity. She never spoke a word, instead she walked to him and kissed him passionately. Trinity unbuckled Nelson's pants and stroked his rock-hard muscle.

"Baby, we can't do this here. Let's go home and get in the bed," He suggested, but Trinity ignored his words.

She dropped to her knees and began to pleasure him with her mouth, first the tip and then inch by inch until he was hitting the back of her throat. His moans and the quivering of his thighs excited her all the more. He grabbed her by the hair and forced himself in and out of her mouth. Without warning, Trinity pushed him away, stood to her feet, and shoved him down into the chair. She straddled him and rode him like an untamed horse. For the first time in years, Trinity's body erupted and her orgasmic juices flowed all over Nelson. Seeing that, feeling that, pushed him to the edge. He stood, bent her over the chair, and feasted on the sweet juices that covered her mound. He then pounded into her until he exploded in her sugar walls.

When Nelson later questioned her, Trinity explained that her best friend saw him when he walked in the door and she knew exactly who had summoned her to the red room. That night was the beginning of a new life for Trinity and Nelson, one that was now filled with a renewed love, passion, and a new respect for the limitless sex that's allowed between a man and his woman.

Leaving Love Behind

Riley settled into her first-class seat on Delta flight 876 to Washington D.C. She'd shipped most of her clothes, shoes, and other personal effects ahead of time to the new apartment the station had rented for her. The furnishings that she and Brandon had purchased together, she'd left behind for him. She still couldn't believe that he wasn't on the plane with her. While she was thrilled about her new opportunity, she was heartbroken to be leaving her love behind.

Riley and Brandon had met in college, both aspired to become journalists. They'd study together and dream about becoming the next big news anchors for major networks. Riley had stayed focused and graduated top of her class, while Brandon had gotten side tracked by the death of his father and the financial issues that followed. Riley had tried to encourage him to at least re-enroll in school part time, but the need to work and help support his mother trumped everything. He took a job as a warehouse worker, performed well and soon moved into a supervisory position. It wasn't what he'd planned, but he was excelling at it and making good money.

Over the last few years, they'd faced many challenges. Riley had lost her sister; Brandon's mom's health had declined quickly, and she passed two years after her husband. Riley hadn't landed the big anchor position she'd hoped for but was instead working as an associate producer for a small, local cable news outlet. She loved what she did, but the money was horrible. But through it all, they stayed together and loved each other through the pain.

Then it happened, Riley got the scoop on a corruption scandal within the Atlanta Mayor's office, but time was of the essence and when there was no field reporter available, Riley jumped in front of the camera and went live with breaking news. The story went national and clips of Riley's report were played all across the country. It wasn't long before the major networks came knocking. But it was D.C. area ABC affiliate, WJLA that came with the offer of Morning News Anchor. It was what Riley had always dreamed about and it came with a contract for more money than she thought she'd ever earn. In addition, the station would pay all her relocation costs and lease her an apartment in Alexandria, a Virginia suburb of the Capital, for a full year. All she needed was for her man to be willing to move with her and she had no doubt that he would.

"Baby, don't get me wrong, I'm happy for you, but my life is here in Atlanta. My job is here, and I will not move out of state just to be unemployed and dependent on my woman. I'm a man and I'm not, nor will I ever be comfortable being supported by you!"

"Brandon, it's just temporary. With your skill set, you'll land a new position in no time."

"That's easy for you to say, you're going to have plenty of money, but when my little bit of savings runs out, I'm screwed. I love you, but I can't move with you, baby!"

"So, you're going to let your macho pride keep us apart? Here I am thinking we've got something special, thinking that we were each other's future."

That was weeks ago. Riley had cried almost every day. Despite her pain, she knew that this was something she had to do. Opportunities like this didn't come along every day. Her flight was uneventful, her bags were waiting at her new high-rise apartment, and she was ready to hit the ground running. By week three, she had found a new favorite coffee shop, settled in at work, and even hanging out periodically with a couple of the girls from work. She and Brandon talked every day, she shared the details of her days and he did the same, but their conversations couldn't compare to the time they used to spend together. Both of them were lonely. After two months of conversation, but not seeing one another, Riley was starting to fear that Brandon either had or would soon have a new girlfriend. Without him, her heart was breaking.

She got up Saturday morning and headed to her coffee shop. She stepped in the door and walked right up to the counter. She hadn't realized that she'd caught the eye of a very handsome man. She didn't feel his eyes burrowing a hole in her back. Anyone that saw him, would see his desire for Riley. He took a couple of deep breaths and decided to make his move. When Riley turned around, she screamed, and tears instantly filled her eyes. Brandon was before her on bended knee.

"Baby, I realize now that my home is wherever you are. I love you, Riley and would be honored if you'd be my wife. Will you marry me, baby?"

"Yes, yes I'll marry you!"

The couple wed eight weeks after Brandon's move to Virginia. He'd secured a management position and they were living the dream.

No Names

Another evening and Carlie found herself at the dinner table eating alone. She knew how important her husband's work was to him. Harper had struggled through grad school while working two mediocre jobs, but it was worth the struggle. Upon graduation, he snagged a position as a junior partner at a large architecture firm. That was two years ago and now it seemed that making partner took precedence over everything, including her. Carlie remembered a time when Harper showered her with affection. They made love like rabbits, christening every room in their house, two and three times over. The sex was unconventional, they were both free spirits that were open to just about anything. But they hadn't been that wild and loose in almost three years. They used to make love at least four days a week, now Carlie was lucky if her husband touched her once every other week. Tears puddled in the corner of her eyes as she recognized the fact that it wasn't just about the sex, it was about the emotional connection, the need to be held, the need to hear her husband sincerely say I love you.

Not long after their marriage, they agreed that if one of them strayed too far off course and began to neglect the other, the neglected one had the option to seek affection from someone else. This was an option that neither had taken advantage of, but it was now a card that Carlie was willing to play. She'd decided that when Harper got home, she would be dressed and ready to go out. She would simply utter their code words, no names, to alert him of her intentions. According to their agreement, he'd have to vacate their home for the night so that she would be free to use it for her much needed one night stand.

Carlie dressed in a seductive black, low cut, mini dress and six-inch heels. With her five feet seven inch, one hundred fifty-pound frame, she would have no problem taking home the man of her choice. It was 9:15 p.m. when Harper finally walked through the door. He looked tired, but still had a smile on his face. When he saw Carlie come around the corner to greet him, his smile grew broader and then dropped to a look of uncertainty.

"Hey baby, did we have plans tonight? Please tell me I didn't forget something big," He pleaded.

"You forgot about me, Harper. You completely forgot about me," Carlie asserted. Then she leaned in, kissed him on the cheek, and whispered, "No names." She then grabbed her keys off the foyer table and walked out the door.

Harper dropped down on the sofa with his head in his hands. How had he allowed

this to happen? For Carlie to play the no names card means that she's been feeling

lonely for quite some time. As he thought about their lives, he realized that he had

been unintentionally neglecting her. A peck on the lips every morning and evening

and an absent minded *I love you* was not sufficient enough to sustain a marriage. His

wife needed to feel wanted, needed to be loved, and he knew how much she craved

sexual satisfaction. It broke his heart that it had come to this, but just as they'd

agreed, he changed clothes, grabbed his keys and vacated the house.

Carlie stepped into her favorite lounge. It was an upscale place with down to earth

people. As she strolled to the bar, she could feel all eyes on her. She took a seat on

one of the available bar stools and smiled at Leslie, the bartender.

"What are you doing here tonight and where is my pretend boyfriend, Harper?"

Leslie asked.

"I needed a break. Been feeling a little neglected and thought I'd take advantage

of an agreement me and Harper made years ago."

"You mean the no names agreement?" Leslie asked with a look of shock.

Leslie and Carlie were actually old friends. They'd met several years ago at a

mutual friend's house warming party and hit it off immediately. Carlie had told her

about the no names option, but Leslie was shocked that she'd actually felt the need to

117

use it. Harper was usually an attentive man who was all about pleasing his woman. Clearly, Carlie felt this was the only way to get his attention.

Sipping on her cocktail, Carlie surveyed the lounge for the man that would make for a suitable hook up. While she saw a couple of really handsome guys, she didn't feel drawn to them. Carlie turned down guy after guy until she saw him. When the six-foot three-inch chocolate drop with the body of a Greek god walked through the door, her heart fluttered, and panties went from dry to moist as all hell. She tried not to look too anxious as he walked towards the bar.

"Excuse me, is this seat taken?" He asked in a sexy alto voice.

"Nope, it's all yours.," Carlie responded in her sexiest voice.

"If I'm not being too forward, may I ask if you're here alone?" The sexy hot guy asked.

"As a matter of fact, I am."

"That's nice to know," He said with a sly grin. "Oh, forgive my manners, I'm—"

"No. No offense, but I really don't want to know your name and I prefer to not give you mine. Is that okay with you?" Carlie asked.

"I suppose so, but may I ask why?" Sexy guy inquired with a raised brow.

"I'm married with no intention of ever leaving my husband. Sadly, we've hit a bump in the road and I seem to be the only one suffering. So, with that said, if you're interested, I'd like to invite you home just for the night. But please be clear, after tonight, I have no plans to ever see you again," Carlie explained.

Sexy guy tossed his drink back, looked at Carlie and said, "Lead the way."

Carlie took a deep breath before crossing the threshold to her home. But as soon as they got in and closed the door, all nerves melted away and they all but attacked each other. Sexy guy took Carlie's face in his hands and kissed her more passionately than she'd been kissed in years. His kisses seductively moved down her neck and he found himself growing excited by her rapid, shallow breaths. He allowed his hands to roam over her body before he unzipped and peeled the dress from her body. He then took a step back and admired every beautiful inch of her.

"Kiss me again," Carlie demanded.

Sexy guy followed her instructions. He kissed her deeply and then left a trail of kisses from her mouth to her panties. Smelling her excitement, touching her dampness made him want to take her hard and fast, but he knew that she was the kind of woman that needed to be loved the right way. Without warning, he lifted her off her feet and she was all too happy to wrap her legs around his waist. He carried her to the sofa where he laid her down and feasted on the sweetness of her love. As he worked his tongue, Carlie threw her head back and moaned her approval. After her first orgasm, sexy guy stood to his feet and removed his clothes. Looking at his physique, Carlie knew she'd made the right decision. He lowered himself down and entered her sugar walls. Each stroke brought them both a little closer to ecstasy. Over the course of the next few hours, he'd moved her from the couch to the table to the floor and ultimately, the bed. She'd not been made love to like this in at least a year.

Sexy guy looked down at Carlie and asked, "How long before I have to leave?"

"You can stay as long as you like. Stay and hold me while I sleep."

"While I'm holding you, can I tell you how beautiful you are and how very much I love you? Can I tell you that I realize how much you deserve the undivided attention of your husband? Can I tell you that I never want to leave you?"

"Only tell me those things if you mean them, Harper. Don't tell them to me now and then slip back into your neglectful behavior. Because while this was a test, the next time I play the no name card, it won't be you that I bring home. And I promise that I'm not threatening you, baby. I love you, but I don't want you to place my love in line behind everything else in your life. I want to be your priority."

"I swear, you are and will forever be my priority," Harper declared as he kissed his wife tenderly. "Now give me some more of that good stuff," He said as he playfully grabbed his wife and let her giggles wash over him.

If You Leave Me Now

Part I ~ All Business

As usual, the bank was bustling with customers trying to get their paychecks

cashed and business owners trying to make deposits. Friday's were always incredibly

busy and that meant that Liz Campbell barely had time to breathe, let alone eat lunch.

She was the Branch Manager and everyone within the bank knew that it was just a

matter of time before she was promoted to Regional Manager. At the ripe old age of

twenty-five, she'd graduated college and hit the ground running. Liz started with the

bank three years ago as a Customer Service Representative and quickly proved that

she was more valuable in a leadership role. As a manager, she was tough but fair with

her employees. As long as they showed up on time, provided excellent customer

service, and followed the policies and procedures of the bank, she was a dream to

work for. But as soon as one of them stepped outside of the lines, she didn't hesitate

to let them know that their job was hanging by a thread.

Liz had just landed another million-dollar deposit account for the bank and was all smiles at the thought of the commission she'd receive for it. No other branch manager had been able to get close to the dollars that she brought in for the organization. This latest account secured her spot at the top of the leader board for the entire southeast region. She was on cloud nine and her joy was contagious. Everyone that encountered her, employees and customers alike, couldn't help but smile and feel uplifted. Her twinkling eyes and gleaming smile added to her already model like appearance. At an even six feet tall in heels, she automatically garnered attention. But her sleek, sexy body, and hot chocolate complexion made her a constant target for sexual overtures and date offers as well as crude remarks. But Liz was focused. The comments didn't faze her, and she had no time to date, she was too busy climbing the corporate ladder.

Leslie Maxwell was a longtime customer of the bank and like clockwork, he came in every Friday at 4:30 p.m. He was a six-foot three-inch tall, lean, fine, handsome specimen of a man. He was also friendly and flirtatious, but that didn't get him far with the women in the bank. He always came in dirty work boots, dingy jeans, and that awful blue D.O.T. work shirt. And while his hair may have been a pool of curls, no one would've ever known it because it was always covered by a baseball cap.

"Here comes your not so secret admirer," whispered Deja, Liz's coworker and friend.

Liz looked up from her desk to see Leslie glide through the bank and tip his dirty cap at her. "Girl please. When I see him, all I can think about is how bad he needs to shower," She remarked.

Deja sat at the desk across from Liz, ready to go over the employee evaluation she'd prepared for one her tellers. "I'm sorry, but I can't agree with that Liz. He may look dirty, but that man always smells so good. I don't know how he does it, but he never smells unpleasant."

"Humph, maybe because all he does for the Department of Transportation is hold the *slow* sign and waive pedestrians through cross walks."

"That's cold, Liz. At least he's working. You know how many men sit up living off of their parents or their women these days? It's ridiculous," Deja said with a scowl on her face.

"And that's one of the reasons I don't date anymore. I refuse to take care of a grown, unemployed, under employed, uneducated, or lazy behind man. I am not the one," Liz replied sharply.

Deja shook her head at her friend's declaration and opened up the file folder she'd

brought into the office with her. She wasn't surprised by what Liz said, she already

knew that was her mindset. Liz was very straight laced and by the book. Everything

in her life had to be just right or not at all. There was no half stepping and no

compromising. Deja knew that even their friendship had certain boundaries. None of

the other employees could know that they socialized outside of work. Within the four

walls of the bank, Deja was just another employee that had to follow the rules or

suffer the consequences. Liz didn't believe in playing favorites, she said that it was

foolish and unprofessional.

As she flipped open the file and spread the paperwork across Liz's mahogany

desk, she looked through the glass partition and straight into Leslie's face. "He's

gorgeous and for all you know, he could be one of the best men that God ever

breathed life into. Don't underestimate him just because of his job," Deja warned.

"If you think he's such a good catch, Deja, then you should go out there and get

him. You two would probably make some beautiful babies," Liz chuckled.

Deja was a beautiful woman. Her caramel complexion, short, sassy haircut, and

adorable dimples garnered her a great deal of compliments. Unfortunately, her size

sixteen frame didn't attract the kind of men that she was attracted to. "Something

tells me that I'm not his type."

"Girl, forget him. We've got work to do. Let me see the review and then we'll discuss little Ms. Thang's future with the bank," Liz chided.

Deja passed Liz her report, already knowing what the outcome for the employee would be. As the head teller, Deja had to be honest in her evaluation. She'd warned the employee multiple times about her tardiness and frequent shortages in her cash drawer. She hated to see the single mother lose her job and had tried to warn her to get her act together. But after verbal and written warnings, the woman still hadn't managed to correct her behavior. Deja was sure that this evaluation was just a formality and she was right. After reading her notes, Liz decided that it was time for the employee to go.

"Will you draw up the termination papers for me please? I'll let her finish the day, but once we lock those doors, her employment with Federal First is over," Liz declared. And just as she'd stated, the woman was let go at the end of the day. Liz was completely unmoved by her pleas for another chance. The woman was escorted out. Liz tied up all her loose ends for the day and left for home.

Part II ~ A Chance Encounter

Liz was slow to get out of bed and start her day. The work week was always so hectic that she spent the first part of her Saturday doing as little as possible. It was her time to sleep in, catch up on her reading, or watch the stories of crazy, murderous people on the I.D. channel. She picked up the remote, but then glanced at the novel she'd been reading and decided that it would be more entertaining than the television. She was fully engrossed in Chase Monet's *Secrets of a Cheating Heart* when her phone rang.

"Hello."

"Hey sexy, what you doing?" Asked the silky, baritone voice.

"Hey Jacob, what are you up to?" Liz asked her dear friend.

"I'm coming over and taking you out for an afternoon of shopping. I just finished moving into my new place and it needs a woman's touch."

"No, you're not. You know that today is my day for relaxation, and shopping is not a relaxing task for me. Plus, the holiday traffic will be crazy. I can't be bothered," Liz declared.

"Girl, get your ass up. You can sleep tomorrow. I'll be over in an hour and you better be ready." Jacob hung up before Liz could get out another objection.

Screeching like an irritated cat, Liz returned her book to the night table, threw the covers back, and dragged herself out of bed. She really wasn't in the mood to shop or decorate, but there wasn't anything she wouldn't do for Jacob. Back in college, it was him that rescued her when some dude tried to date rape her. It was Jacob that drove her to her parent's house and pulled her dad off of her mom and kept him from killing her. It was him that consoled her and got her through her first broken heart. It's always been Jacob and she knew that he'd always be there for her. And for that reason, she'd always be there for him.

Like clockwork, Jacob banged on her door an hour after their phone conversation. Liz stomped to the door and yanked it open. "Haven't I told you about banging on the door like some mad man," She exclaimed.

Jacob chuckled as he glided his thick, sculpted frame though the door. He was a handsome man and he knew it. His low cut, wavy hair, smooth, white chocolate complexion, and muscular body attracted attention everywhere they went. And despite the Caucasian sisters that threw themselves at him, he'd always gravitated to women of color. Jacob often joked that he was addicted to their melanin rich skin.

"Woman, stop your bitchin' and moanin' and give me a hug," He laughed as he closed the door and wrapped Liz up in a bear hug.

"OMG, man let me go before you break me in half," Liz laughed as she wiggled from his clutches.

127

"Have you eaten?"

"Now why would I eat when I know that you're going to feed me," Liz teased. "And I want something good! Don't try to take me to Waffle House today or I swear I'll pick out the most jacked up crap for your new place. It'll be so hideous that you'll never get a decent woman to stay over."

"You are so wrong. There's nothing wrong with Waffle House, but don't worry, we're headed to brunch at The Ritz. I just landed a few new clients and you're now looking at the trainer to the stars."

"Seriously? Dude, this is great. Let me grab my bag and you can tell me all about it in the car."

Jacob gleamed with excitement as he told Liz all about how great the booming film industry in Atlanta had been for business. His gym was always packed and with word of mouth about his upscale décor, top notch equipment, and unique classes, he'd gotten several requests from major actors and actresses for personal training sessions. Jacob's pockets were finally full, and he couldn't be happier.

They laughed and talked while enjoying the delicious brunch. Liz's stomach was full and all she really wanted was to go back home and climb back into her bed. But instead, she thanked Jacob for the meal, and asked if he had a particular furniture store in mind.

"I figured we could hit a couple of little neighborhood stores and maybe go to Kirkland's for the accessories."

"You just leased an expensive high-rise apartment in downtown Atlanta, we will not furnish it with cheap, neighborhood store furniture. How about we start at Ethan Allan? Hello, do you hear me talking to you?" Liz snapped her fingers in Jacob's face. When he continued to stare off to the left, Liz turned to see who had put her friend in a trance. When her eyes met those of his target, a broad smile crossed her face and she trotted off with open arms to greet Deja.

"Hey girl, what are you doing here?" Liz asked as she hugged her friend who was waiting to be seated.

"This is my monthly treat. The brunch here is incredible and we both know that I'd starve waiting for my Prince Charming to show up and bring me here," Deja laughed.

Jacob strolled over and stood by Liz's side. He was completely captivated by Deja's beauty and patiently waited for Liz to make an introduction. When she kept chattering, he nudged her and cleared his throat. "Don't you think you should introduce me to your lovely friend?" He finally interrupted.

"Oh, I'm sorry. Deja, this is my dear friend, Jacob. Jacob, this is my friend and coworker, Deja."

Jacob took Deja's hand in his. "It's a pleasure to meet you and please forgive me if this is too forward, but you are absolutely beautiful."

Deja blushed and could hardly believe that he was talking to her. She was a confident woman, very self-assured, but the men that usually approached her were not quite as fit, not quite as handsome, and were never white. "It's nice to meet you as well," She smiled as she gently pulled her hand from his grasp. "Liz, you didn't tell me you were out on a date." Deja wanted to be sure that she wasn't flirting with her friend's man. She refused to ever be one of those back stabbing, steal your man kind of women.

"Girl please, while Jacob is a dear friend, he is not, nor will he ever be my man," Liz chuckled. "I wish I had known you were coming here, we could've all eaten together. I hate that you're dining alone."

"It's no big deal, I do it all the time. I'm not the type the woman that has to have a dinner companion in order to enjoy fine dining."

"I love the high level of self-confidence I'm getting from you," Jacob interjected. "And I know that you planned on dining alone, but I'd love to join you. That's if you don't mind a little company."

"But we just ate," Liz grunted.

"But I didn't have dessert and their coffee is delicious," Jacob said as he gave Liz a glance that screamed for her to shut up. He turned his attention back to Deja, "So, what do you say, mind if I join you?"

"Not at all," Deja blushed.

"Liz, you can take my car on home and I'll grab a cab and head your way when we're done," He offered as he practically threw the keys at Liz.

"Well damn, guess I'll run some errands and go back home. You crazy kids have fun."

After Liz left, she rode around to a couple of furniture stores to try and get some ideas for Jacob's new place. She found a beautiful but manly living room and dining set at Haverty's that she would try and convince him to get. Her last stop was by Whole Foods. She'd been meaning to go grocery shopping and now was as good a time as any. She whipped the car into a parking space near the back of the lot. She could use the walk plus she wanted to ensure that nothing happened to Jacob's car on her watch. She strolled through the aisles picking up items here and there. Her last stop would be produce, but as she headed in that direction, something caught her eye and the distraction caused her to crash her cart into the cart of another shopper.

"Oh, my goodness, I'm so sorry. I should've been paying attention," Liz apologized as she looked up into the face of the most gorgeous man she'd ever seen. His curly hair and hazel eyes made her heart flutter.

"Liz, is that you? I've never seen you outside of your work environment. How are you today?"

"I'm fine," Liz stammered as she tried to place the gorgeous face. Then it hit her and like a pin sticking a balloon, she was completely deflated. "Oh, hi Mr. Maxwell, I almost didn't recognize you without your work clothes and baseball cap. How are today?" She asked flatly.

"I'm great and please, call me Leslie."

"Okay, Leslie. Well, it was good seeing you, take care and I'll see you in the bank next Friday."

Liz tried to rush off, but Leslie placed his hand on her buggy. "I know you're a busy woman, but would you please allow me to buy you a cup of coffee? There's a Starbucks next door. We could grab an outside table and enjoy the beautiful fall weather and a brief conversation."

"Oh, I don't think so, Leslie. I should probably get this stuff home and put away."

Leslie chuckled, "You only have five items in your buggy and none of them are perishable. Really, I promise not to keep you long."

Liz finally gave in, paid for her items, and walked with Leslie to the coffee shop. She warned him that she only had a few minutes to spare. Despite how handsome he was, she decided that he was only worth about five minutes of her time and that was all she planned to give him. But an hour later, Liz was still at the table wrapped up in everything that fell from his lips. She listened as he talked about being raised by a single parent. Ovarian cancer took his mother when he was only seven and as hard as his grandmother fought to have the privilege to raise him, his father refused. He declared that only a man could properly raise a boy to be a man. Leslie did get to spend three weeks of every summer with his grandmother in upstate New York. But his thoughts, behaviors and priorities were all shaped by his father. When Liz asked where the name Leslie came from, he explained that it was his mother's middle name and she'd always wanted her child to share her name.

When Leslie turned the tables, and began to ask about Liz's childhood, she began to freeze up. Liz only shared that she was raised in a two-parent home, had a strained relationship with her father and wanted to be better than her mother, but she refused to say why. The last thing Leslie wanted was to push her away, so he changed the subject and told her how much he admired her position at the bank and her obvious strong work ethic. Liz blushed and timidly asked him why he chose to work for the D.O.T.

"What can I say, I'm a man that likes to work with his hands. I also hate gyms and this work provides great exercise for me. It keeps me fit," Leslie explained.

Their conversation continued as the afternoon breeze began to pick up. The sun was still shinning, and the atmosphere was light as they chatted and watched all the smiling faces passing by. Liz checked her watch and was shocked that the five-minute limit that turned into an hour had somehow transformed into two hours. "Oh goodness, I've got to get out of here. I'm in my friend's car and he'll be calling any minute to see where I am."

"I understand. May I walk you to the car?"

"Of course," Liz conceded.

The laughter and teasing continued as they slow strolled to the car. Liz unlocked the door and before she could ease into the seat, Leslie smoothly stated, "Thank you for spending a little time with me. I really enjoyed myself."

"So, did I, Leslie, it was time well spent."

"So, what do you say we do it again? I'd love to take you out on an official date. I know a great little Moroccan restaurant, we could sip a little wine, try some new dishes and be entertained by belly dancers."

"Dude, are you seriously trying to take me to a strip club?" Liz asked with a twisted face.

"Of course not," Leslie laughed. "It really is like a little show and they even get guests to dance with them. It's quite entertaining. What do you say, let's experience something new?"

"I tell you what, give me your number and let me think about it. If I decide to go, I'll call you. If I decide against it, I'll see you in the bank on Friday."

"Fair enough." Leslie gave Liz a business card with his number as she slid into the car. He closed the door and watched as she drove away.

Part III ~ Decisions

Deja turned over and faced the wall, unable to wrap her brain around what had just happened. *Maybe I dreamed it*. The strong arm that Jacob wrapped around her waist as he moved closer confirmed that she'd not been dreaming. After Liz left them at The Ritz, they enjoyed great conversation while indulging in the fabulous cuisine. It was as if they'd known each other for years. And while the connection was great, the sparks were undeniable. Each time that Jacob reached out and touched her hand, it was as if someone set off a little jolt of electricity inside her. Finally, after a couple of mimosas, Jacob worked up the nerve to ask her if she were willing to take their date to a more private location. Naïvely, Deja agreed thinking that they would head to a smaller, less congested venue. But Jacob excused himself and when he returned, he had a key to a suite upstairs in the hotel.

Deja wrestled with her decision to follow him upstairs until he closed the door behind them. She was a good girl and had never done anything like this before. She kept debating, asking herself 'Do I leave now? Am I really going to allow this to happen?' But then Jacob caressed her face, kissed her full, wanting lips and she dismissed all thoughts of leaving. It had been a long time since she'd felt the strong hand of a man and she decided that regardless of the outcome, she was going to enjoy the moment. She let Jacob's kisses wash away her fears and inhibitions. His tongue tasted so good in her mouth. Her body tensed up as he began to unbutton the cardigan sweater that covered her ample bosom.

"You are so beautiful," He whispered, and she was immediately put at ease. "I want to taste every inch of you," He moaned, and tingles took over every erogenous zone on her body. "I need to feel you," he confessed and her panties got a little bit wetter.

Jacob removed her bra, allowing her full breasts to slightly drop and he tried to catch every bit of them in his mouth. He moved from one to the other, sucking her nipples until they became completely erect with excitement. He unhooked the waistband of her skirt and allowed it to drop to the floor. Deja thought she'd become bashful or uncomfortable when he stepped back to visually take in her naked glory. But the way he looked at her only excited her more. She stepped forward and helped him out of his shirt. Jacob's sculpted body sent a small trickle of joy on a journey down her inner thigh. He reached down and slid his fingers between her legs and what he felt made his soldier stand at full attention. He ushered her over to the bed, laid her down and rested his face between her thighs. Deja's mind was blown as he licked, sucked, and fingered her to that happy place she'd not visited in years. Unable to control herself, her joy squirted out all over him and Jacob lapped it up like a dog drinking water.

"Please tell me you have a condom," Deja whispered. Jacob hastily reached for his pants and pulled a Magnum out of his wallet. Like magic, his soldier was covered and diving deep into her new territory. He plunged in and out, in and out, in and out until Deja thought she'd lose her mind. When she released on him again, Jacob lifted her legs to his shoulders, giving himself even more access to the deepest part of her. A few more thrusts and he released his troops into the confinements of the rubber that hopefully survived the intense encounter.

Jacob stroked her body and asked, "Are you okay? You got quiet and turned your back, should I be worried?"

"No, I'm fine, just digesting what we did. I can't imagine what you must think. I mean we literally just met. What in the world will Liz think?"

"Let me first say that this is none of Liz's business, we're consenting adults and this is just between us. It doesn't matter if we met ten minutes ago or ten years ago, we have an undeniable connection and I'm excited about spending more time with you. I think that this was all meant to be," He confessed as he sweetly kissed her shoulder.

They stayed in the hotel room talking, sexing, and eating until Sunday morning. Deja learned how good it could be to let go and live in the moment, no matter how erotic that moment was. When they finally dressed and left, Deja dropped Jacob off at his apartment and ran home to change before rushing to Liz's house. She'd never had an encounter like that before and she certainly didn't want Liz finding out from Jacob. She wanted to share it with her friend, and make sure that Liz wouldn't think ill of her or be angered by the hook up of her friends.

"What are you doing here, girl? I thought you'd be in church," Liz said as she opened the door for her unexpected guest.

"I need to be in church," Deja confessed. "I'm sorry for showing up unannounced, but I really needed to talk to you."

"Come on in. Is everything okay? You look really upset."

"Actually, I feel amazing, but I am concerned about our friendship," Deja admitted. "I just need to make sure that we're good."

"Why wouldn't we be good? Wait, is this about Jacob staying at The Ritz with you?"

"Well, yes…" Deja's voice trailed off as she dropped her head.

Laughing at her needless concern, Liz ushered Deja into the kitchen, put on a pot of coffee, and put her friend at ease. "Deja, there has never been anything between me and Jacob except a great friendship. He's an awesome guy and, I actually think that the two of you would make a great couple. I'm just annoyed with myself for not thinking of hooking y'all up months ago."

"I know that you two are only friends, but a little more than just brunch happened yesterday. We ended up getting a room and stayed the night. I literally left The Ritz two hours ago. I ran home, showered, dressed, and came straight here."

"Oh my gosh, you and Jacob spent the night together? Y'all did the wild monkey dance?" Liz asked as she moved her fingers to gesture a sex act.

With concern etched across her face, Deja confirmed her thoughts. "Yes, we did. I swear Liz, we did it all."

"Well, why are you looking like that? Was it that bad?"

"Just the opposite, Liz, it was incredible! I have never experienced a sexual encounter like that before. That man sent shock waves through my body. I swear there are parts of me that are still tingling. And he made me feel beautiful, Liz. He wasn't turned off by my weight. As a matter of fact, my size seemed to turn him on."

"Wow, you are seriously gushing over this man."

"Just don't be mad about this hook up. I'm sure he'll tell you all about it, but I wanted to tell you first," Deja said.

"Well he came by here earlier to get his car and he didn't mention a thing. But now I know why he was in the same clothes he had on yesterday," Liz chuckled. "But no worries, Deja, if you guys are happy then I'm happy."

"Thank you, Liz. He did make me happy, I just hope that the first time I was with him won't be the last time I'm with him."

"Jacob is not that kind of guy. He would never allow himself to be intimate with you if he had no intentions of creating a relationship with you," Liz assured her. "But on another note, guess what I did yesterday after I left you guys."

"I give, what did you do?"

"Went to Whole Foods where I literally bumped into Leslie, that guy from the bank."

"Aww hell, please tell me you were civil to the poor guy?"

"I was civil to him for about two hours over coffee."

"What! You actually spent time with him?"

"Yes, I did, and it was so nice. We sat outside of the Starbucks beside the grocery store, sipped coffee and talked. He's actually a really nice man. And my goodness, he's so handsome when he's all cleaned up. I swear I could sit and run my fingers through his hair all day."

"So, did y'all make plans to see each other again?" Deja quizzed.

"He asked me out to some Moroccan place. I took his number and told him I'd think about it."

"Where's his number?"

Liz picked the card up from the counter where she'd left it last night. Twiddled it between her fingers and passed it on to Deja. "The one thing I can't figure out is why his information is on such an elegant card with that business name when he works for the D.O.T?"

Deja inspected the card, read the name Wellscore Construction and surmised that he actually worked for one of those subcontracting companies that do work for the D.O.T. Her explanation sounded plausible to Liz. "Now that we've figured that out, you are going to call him and go out on that date, right?"

"I don't know. You know how I like to stay focused on work," Liz explained.

"No, you like to avoid the possibility of being hurt. I understand how your father's abuse of your mother impacted you. I realize that your college sweetheart completely broke your heart, but it's time for you to move on. You need to give yourself chance at a life filled with a successful career *and* an abundance of love. He's clearly a decent guy, give him and the possibility of love a chance."

Part IV ~ Tonight I Give In

Two months had passed since Liz gave in and began dating Leslie. They had spent every weekend together since that first date. He'd opened her heart and filled it with a pure, sincere love. Every flower he'd sent, note he'd written and kiss he'd planted on her lips confirmed his love for her. And despite her best efforts to hold back, she'd returned love to him. Pure, unadulterated love. The only thing she hadn't given him was her body, but that would all change tonight. Liz had prepared a meal of grilled salmon, baked potatoes, and sautéed green beans. She'd even made a good attempt at his favorite dessert, chocolate lava cake. She nervously jumped out the shower, put lotion on her body, and slipped on a sexy negligée. She turned to check herself in the mirror when she heard the doorbell ring. A scantily clad woman serving him food was one of Leslie's fantasies and starting tonight, she was going to try and make all his fantasies come true. She slipped on a pair of six inch heels and trotted off to let Leslie in.

Leslie entered the candle lit house, smelled the food, and knew that he was in for treat. But when Liz closed the door and stepped out so that he could see her, his jaw dropped. He'd been careful not to pressure Liz. He wanted her to be comfortable with taking the next step, and boy was he glad he hadn't rushed her. She looked

phenomenal. Instantly he thought *to hell with dinner, I just want to eat her.* But he

was determined to let her lead.

"I hope you're hungry," Liz asked as she planted a soft kiss on his lips.

"For you, I'm starved. For food, yeah, I could eat," He joked.

Liz led him to his seat in the dining room and then began to place dinner on the

table. For Leslie, it was like punishment watching her strut around with all of her

goods on display. Just looking at her glide across the floor with her skin shimmering

in the candle light had him hard as a rock. He wanted to devour her, but instead he sat

across from her and ate his food like a good boy.

"The food was really good, babe. Thank you for doing all of this for me."

"You're welcome, love. I also made your favorite desert. Would you like it now

or later?" Liz asked as she removed the dishes from the table and slightly turned up

the seductive music she had playing in the background.

"How about we wait a little while on dessert?" Leslie responded in hopes of

getting another kind of treat. He was not disappointed when Liz came over and

straddled him in his chair. Facing him, she began to plant sweet, soft kisses on his

lips. But feeling his growing manhood, she became more excited and her kisses

intensified. Unintentionally, she began to slow grind in his lap. His moans and

ravenous kisses were driving her crazy. Liz stood and motioned for him to stand as well. She led Leslie by the hand down the long hall to her bedroom. Once inside, she encouraged Leslie to undress and he was more than happy to oblige. She pushed him back on the bed, straddled him again, but this time she moved down his body until her mouth found what it had been longing for. She took his manhood into her mouth. First the head, swirling her tongue all around it. Then slowly she took more and more of him in. Her hand firmly went up and down his shaft while her head followed. When she felt his body tense, she slowly moved back up, lifted herself and gently guided him in. She rode Leslie as if she were a rodeo star and he was a prize bull. He caressed her back and breasts as she moved up and down. He sat up, nibbled on her nipples and flipped her on her back. Liz moaned and squealed as Leslie plunged in deeper and deeper until they both exploded in ecstasy.

It had been three years since Liz allowed a man to touch her intimately and she was so glad that Leslie was the one to touch her both physically and emotionally. They spent the night in each other's arms sharing their hopes and dreams for the future. Liz smiled bashfully as Leslie made it known that he wanted his future to include her. He told her how he'd imagined them building a life together and raising a family. She fell asleep with the words "I love you," echoing in her ear. It couldn't have been more perfect.

The alarm blared and Liz banged the top of it to try and shut it off. The last thing in the world she wanted was to leave Leslie's arms, but it was a work day and they both had to get a move on. Leslie caressed and kissed her shoulder.

"I don't want to leave you, babe. I'll call in if you will," He offered.

"I wish I could, but my supervisor is scheduled to come in for a meeting today. I'm sorry, but I've got to go."

"I understand," He said as he pulled himself from bed and began to put his clothes on. "If I'm going to be on time, I guess I better run home, shower and get dressed for work."

"You can always shower here," Liz said.

"Thanks babe, but I don't have any clean clothes here. Besides, I need my uniform."

"I know, I just thought I'd offer."

"Well, how about this for an offer. Let's go away for the weekend. I'll rent a car and we'll head to Amelia Island. It'll be the perfect weekend getaway. What do you think?" Leslie asked with his voice full of hope.

"That sounds perfect, Leslie. Once I get settled in at work, I'll make us a hotel reservation at one of the beach resorts."

"No, no, don't you worry about a thing. I'll take care of everything," Leslie assured. "Now come on and lock the door behind me."

They strolled to the door and gave each other a warm hug goodbye. Liz stood in the doorway wrapped in a sheet and watched as her man crossed the neighborhood street to get to his car. He turned around to blow her one last kiss when a speeding car barreled down the street and hit him. The impact threw Leslie in the air and he hit the pavement with a thud. The driver kept going and in what seemed like slow motion, Liz ran screaming from the house.

Part V ~ If You Leave Me Now

One of the neighbors that witnessed the horrific incident called 911 and ran to be by Liz's side while they waited on help. Liz sobbed and begged Leslie to stay with her. "Please babe, look at me, stay with me! Oh God, please, please let him be okay," She cried. The neighbor ran into Liz's house and grabbed a house coat and a pair of slippers she saw at the foot of her bed and rushed them out to her.

"Here honey, put these on. The ambulance and police will be here any minute and you don't need to let them see you wrapped in a sheet," the woman advised as she helped an almost inconsolable Liz into the lounge wear. And just as she'd said, the cop car, ambulance and fire truck came blaring down the street as soon as she slipped the other shoe on. The paramedics rushed to Leslie's side and the neighbor had to drag a still sobbing Liz back so that they'd have room to work on him.

A short but well-toned cop approached the women. "Ladies, can you please tell me what happened?"

Liz managed to control her crying long enough to tell the officer about the black Acura TLS that sped down the street and tossed Leslie in the air. She shook her head in dismay as she explained that the car didn't even stop. But the neighbor did advise

that the driver slowed down enough for her to get the custom license plate.

"Did you write it down?" The cop asked.

"No, there was no need," She explained. "I'm not sure of the state, but the plate

read SPEEDER."

"Thank you, ma'am, this vital piece of information will go a long way in tracking

down the perpetrator."

Liz watched on as the paramedics assessed Leslie. But when one yelled for the

defibrillator, she lost it all over again. She was consumed with fear as they tried to

jolt his heart and regain a pulse. She let out a sigh of relief when she heard them say

that they'd gotten him back, but had to get him to the trauma center. They loaded him

into the ambulance and told her that she could meet them at Grady Memorial

Hospital. Liz ran into her house and quickly threw on some jeans, a t-shirt and some

sneakers. She grabbed her cell phone, purse and keys and ran right back out the door.

To Liz's surprise, the same neighbor was standing by her car waiting for her.

"You're in no condition to drive. I'll drop you off on my way to work."

Liz jumped in the car and they pulled off. "I can't thank you enough for all that

you've done," Liz said. "I honestly don't know what I would've done if you hadn't

been there."

"You're welcome. I'd hope that if the tables were turned you'd do the same for me."

"Of course, I would. And please forgive me, but I don't even know your name," Liz sniffed.

"I'm Cecily Connors and please don't feel bad, I've only been in the house a week." In an effort to keep her calm, Cecily continued to engage Liz in idle conversation. The ride to Grady seemed to take forever when in fact, it only took about twenty minutes. Cecily pulled up to the emergency entrance and passed Liz her business card. "Call me if you need me," She offered. Liz thanked her for everything and Cecily waited until Liz disappeared into the hospital before pulling off.

The nurse assured Liz that they were doing all they could for Leslie. She then passed Liz a bag containing everything that was in Leslie's pants pockets. Silent tears fell as Liz opened his cell phone and prepared to call his dad and deliver the news of what had happened. After she cried her way through that call, she dialed work, gave her assistant manager instructions on what needed to be taken care of and asked to be transferred to Deja. When she heard her friend's voice, she completely fell apart. After hearing about the accident, Deja gathered her things and rushed off to be at Liz's side. It wasn't long before Leslie's father, Gary, and Deja came rushing through the doors.

"Have you heard anything?" Gary asked anxiously.

"No, they're still working on him. The nurse promised to keep me updated." Liz went on to explain to them exactly what had happened. As she recounted the events, tears began to once again stream down her face. Gary's eyes also welled with tears and Deja did her best to comfort them both. They continued to nervously wait and finally a doctor approached them with news about Leslie. Sadly, he was in critical condition with a serious brain injury. The broken bones would heal, but the brain injury was the cause of great concern.

"The next twenty-four to forty-eight hours are critical," The doctor explained. "We've put a shunt in his head which will drain the excess fluid and hopefully decrease the swelling. If that happens, then he'll have a great chance at a full recovery. If it doesn't, we'll be looking at a more extensive surgery with a rather unpredictable outcome."

Liz sobbed in Deja's arms. "Can we please see him?"

"Yes, I can permit two of you back into the ICU unit, but only for a brief time. Keep in mind that he's hooked up to a lot of tubes and machines, but it's all to help us accurately access his situation from minute to minute," The doctor explained.

"We understand," Gary acknowledged as the doctor led him and Liz to Leslie's room. Liz steadied herself on Gary's arm. The doctor had not lied. It looked as if Leslie was hooked up to every machine ever created. Gary released Liz's arm and moved to his son's bedside. "You're a fighter son," He said as he placed his hand on

Leslie's shoulder. "You are a fighter and I know that you can survive this. You just have to decide that you want to. I love you son and I'll be right here when you wake up." Gary stepped back, kissed Liz on the forehead and said, "I'm going to step out and let you have a moment alone with him." Gary then left the room as he wiped tears from his eyes.

Liz stepped to the bed and took Leslie's hand in hers. "You said you loved me this morning, but you didn't get to hear me say that I love you too, and I do, Leslie, I swear I do. I love every curly strand of hair on your head, every smile that settles on your lips, and your silly sense of humor. I love you with my whole heart, Leslie. But if you leave me now, we'll never know what an incredible life we could have. We'll never meet the beautiful children that we could create, we'll never get the chance to grow old together and annoy the hell out of each other," She said as she caressed his hand. "And I want all of those things, Leslie, but I only want them with you. So, I need you to wake up, babe. I need you to wake up and love me."

Part VI ~ The Good And The Bad

Against everyone's advice, Liz stayed at the hospital day and night. She'd sent Deja to her house to pack some things for her and she'd taken family leave from her job. The furthest Liz would venture away from Leslie's side was to the cafeteria. It had truly been the longest three days of her life. She was exhausted mentally and physically, but felt that Leslie's chances of recovery were greatly increased if he could feel her presence, and she was right. Sitting in a chair with her head laying on the edge of the bed, she didn't see his eyes flutter open. She didn't notice when he was finally able to focus on her or when he wiggled his mouth trying to figure out why that ventilator tube was down his throat. But she did feel something tickle her head. When she raised up and saw Leslie looking back at her, tears of joy danced on the rim of her eyes.

"Babe, you're awake. Thank God, you're awake," Liz praised. Leslie slowly raised his hand towards the tube in his mouth. "No, no, don't pull that out. Let me get the doctor, babe." She turned to get help and was greeted at the door by his doctor and nurse. "He's awake," She gushed.

The doctor stepped over to his bedside to do an evaluation. "You gave us quite a scare, Mr. Maxwell. I'm so glad to see that you're awake and alert." Leslie reached

153

for the tube again as he wiggled his mouth. "Is that tube bothering you?" Leslie nodded his head. "That's a good sign, but we can't remove it quite yet." The doctor and nurse maneuvered around the bed, checking Leslie's vitals, listening to his lungs, and checking his response to stimuli. Leslie's pupils reacted to the light, his limbs jerked when that metal wheel was rolled against them. "You sir are a very lucky man. So far, everything is looking good, but we're going to send you for another MRI of your head before we decrease the ventilator and ultimately remove it, okay?" Leslie nodded yes. The doctor patted his hand, pleased that his patient appeared to be on the road to a full recovery.

Over the course of the next two days, the shunt was removed from Leslie's head and he was taken off of the ventilator. And aside from a slight limp, he would in fact make a complete recovery. Liz and Gary rejoiced over Leslie's miraculous recovery as well as the fact that his assailant had been arrested. There was so much to be thankful for. Truly a Christmas miracle.

"So, son, I talked to the doctor earlier," Gary said. "The good news is that you'll likely go home tomorrow. The bad news is that with that sling on your arm and cast on your leg, you can't stay alone. I've arranged for you to stay at the house and I've hired a nursing agency to provide round the clock care."

"Oh gracious, that's going to be so expensive," Liz interjected.

"He can afford it," Gary chuckled.

Liz looked at Leslie with doubt. *Does he know what you do for a living?* "Gary, he is certainly welcome to stay with me. I'd be honored to nurse him back to health," She said as she winked at Leslie. "I can continue my leave for a while and hire a nurse to come in an hour or so a day to help with bath time," Liz generously offered.

"Dad, would you excuse us for a moment? I need to clear some things up with Liz."

His father nodded, knowing the conversation that Leslie was about to have. Gary exited the room and gently closed the door.

Leslie sighed deeply as he reached out for Liz's hand. "Baby, I haven't been completely honest with you. I allowed you to think one thing when my situation is quite different."

"What are you talking about, Leslie?" Liz asked with a look of confusion etched across her face.

"Yes, I enjoy working with my crew. I like getting my hands dirty and the street work is a great way for me to stay in shape, but it's not something that I have to do. I wasn't completely honest with you when you asked about my business card. Yes, the company is a sub-contractor for the D.O.T., but what I didn't say is that I own that company. Wellscore Construction is a very successful company that I established five years ago. Since then, it's grown by leaps and bounds and is now worth a few million dollars."

155

"You have got to be kidding?" Liz asked in disbelief. "Why didn't you tell me? Did you think I was a gold digger or something?"

"Absolutely not, but you initially seemed so uninterested in me. I've been hurt before and my feelings for you run so deep that it would've been incredibly easy for you to hurt me as well. I just wanted to wait until I was sure of your feelings for me before I told you. Please don't be mad, baby."

Confused, Liz asked, "Well if you just work for the hell of it, why do you come into the bank to deposit a check every week?"

"If you look at that account closely, you'll see that I'm not on it alone. I deposit that money for a family that I help support. The husband is a disabled veteran and they had an incredibly hard time trying to juggle their living expenses and his medical bills. Putting money in that account is my way of saying thanks for all he's done and sacrificed for our country," Leslie explained. "Please tell me you're not angry with me?"

Liz chuckled and looked at Leslie warmly. "I completely understand, babe. I probably would've done the same thing," She confessed as she caressed his hand. "But this news doesn't change the fact that I'm more than happy to nurse you back to health."

"Thank you, baby. That good heart of yours, your generosity, love and kindness, it all makes me love you more. It's part of the reason that I want to marry you," Leslie admitted as he pulled a little blue box from under the covers. He opened the box to reveal a five-carat engagement ring from Tiffany's. "Please tell me that you'll be my wife?"

Part VII ~ And Here We Are

The kids giggled like they'd just pulled off the greatest caper of all time. Lauren didn't think that her mom saw her sneak the chocolate chips off the counter and share them with her little brother, Levi. The chocolate chips that she was supposed to be adding to the cookie batter she instead added to her mouth. But Liz played along for a moment and allowed the kids to indulge in a few of the chips before she feigned shock and surprise.

"Lauren, you sneaky little thing! How many of those chocolate chips have you two eaten?" Liz asked with a raised eyebrow.

"I only had one, Mommy, but Levi ate thirty!"

"Thirty? I don't think his belly could hold thirty chocolate chips," Liz giggled as she looked at her two-year old son holding his hand out for more. "Okay, no more chocolate chips for you guys. I've got to finish these cookies before our guests start to arrive. Lauren, take your brother to the bathroom and when you come out I want you guys to have clean hands and faces. Y'all can watch television in the play room until everyone gets here."

"Yes, ma'am. Come on, Levi," Lauren said as she led him towards the back.

Liz filled the chafing dishes on the buffet table with rice, beans, seasoned beef, chicken, and tortillas. Serving bowls were filled with shredded cheese, sour cream, tomatoes, onions, guacamole, and salsa. The finishing touch would be Liz's famous double chocolate chip cookies. Just as she placed the last bowl on the buffet, Leslie came rushing through the door.

"Babe, you look a dirty mess. I thought you weren't going to work on the road today?" Liz quipped.

"I got bored behind the desk, plus I hadn't had a decent work-out in a while. I needed to move, to be active," He explained as he gently pecked his wife on the lips.

"I hear you, but now I need for you to hurry and take a quick shower and dress. You know that our company will be arriving any minute."

"I'll hurry, but those jokers aren't company, they're family." Leslie laughed as he took the steps two at a time.

Liz thanked God every day that Leslie was able to make a full recovery from that hit and run accident. Seven years later and the only physical evidence of it was the slight limp that they already knew he'd be left with. But it hadn't slowed him down one bit. Within two years of Leslie being discharged from the hospital, the driver of the car had been convicted and sentenced. They had their dream destination wedding in Hawaii and found out that they were going to be parents. Liz felt that she was truly living a dream life. Aside from the love of God, she'd received more love than she ever even knew existed. Her life got better with the passing of each year.

The doorbell rang and the kids immediately came running from the back. Levi did his best to keep up with his big sister. "Mommy, they're here, they're here," Lauren squealed.

"Well come on, let's let them in," Liz laughed heartily. She swung the door open and was almost trampled by Deja and Jacob's twin boys, David and Daniel. "Really, y'all are just going to run past me like that?"

Hey Auntie Liz," They sang in unison as they literally threw themselves around her legs. Liz hugged them back and smiled as her two little ones showered Jacob and Deja with hugs and kisses.

"Hey, where's my love?" Leslie asked as he descended the stairs. The four kids swarmed him like bees. When they finally let him go and ran to the play-room, he greeted Jacob and Deja. "Come on in guys. Liz has put out quite a spread and I for one can't wait to dig in. What can I get y'all to drink?"

"I love this, Liz, a Mexican themed pre-Christmas dinner!" Deja was blown away by the ten foot Christmas tree and all the other holiday decorations. But she was most pleased with the buffet. Deja didn't care for the traditional dinner, she'd always said that it bored her. Jacob found that to be another endearing quirk of Deja's. In all honesty, there wasn't anything about her that he hadn't found a way to love. He loved her kind heart, beautiful features, and full figure. But most of all, he loved her for the gift of his kids. Who would have imagined that their first encounter would have left her pregnant? They thought that they were being careful, but that condom that Jacob whipped out of his wallet in The Ritz hotel room had torn. Deja was terrified that he'd think she gotten pregnant on purpose. She never imagined that he'd jump for joy. Three months after their initial meeting, they stood before the Justice of the Peace and exchanged vows. Neither had time to worry that it all happened too fast, they were too busy being happy.

While Leslie poured everyone a glass of wine, Liz went to open the door for the last guests to arrive. She greeted Cecily and her new boyfriend, Caleb, with warm hugs. Liz was so moved by all that Cecily had done to help her and Leslie during and after the accident. She realized that people like Cecily didn't come along every day and felt honored to call her friend.

The couples and their children laughed, ate, played board games, and gave thanks for their friendship. Liz looked across the table at her husband. Her heart was so full of love for him and their kids. Her heart was full of love for God and the fact that He hadn't allowed Leslie to leave her.

After The Storm

Torrey stood in the endless line behind the other last-minute shoppers who'd been scared into stockpiling water, food, and batteries in preparation for the storm the of century. Truth be told, Torrey only had a couple of bottles of wine, a loaf of bread, a jar of peanut butter, and a bottle of jelly in her cart. She figured the storm could only last so long and why buy up a bunch of crap that would either go bad if they lost electricity or be ruined if it flooded. Finally, after a ten-minute wait, she paid for her items, jumped in her car and headed home.

As she maneuvered through the city streets, her cell phone rang…again. "Mama, my mind is made up, I'm staying at home. No matter how many times you call me, my response is going to be the same. I'm staying home," She explained without even a hello.

"I know you want to stay at home baby, but Savannah is supposed to get hit pretty hard. Please come on back to Vidalia with me and your dad or I'll literally worry myself to death. You don't want to be the cause of my demise, do you?"

Torrey couldn't help but laugh. "Mama, your guilt trip, albeit good, is not going to work. I have plenty of bottled water at home, I just left the grocery store with nonperishable food, I've got candles, and both my phones are fully charged. I'm going to be fine."

"What if your building floods?" Her mom asked out of desperation.

"Mom, I'm on the third floor, above the parking garage. It would have to rain for forty days and forty nights before the water reached my condo. I'm going to be fine. I love you, tell Dad that I love him, and I'll check on y'all later this evening." Torrey disconnected the call and whipped into a parking space.

Looking around, she was surprised to see the garage almost empty. Apparently, most of her neighbors opted to abandon ship. But that didn't scream "warning" for Torrey. For her it just meant peace and quiet. She gathered her grocery bag, purse, and laptop and headed towards the elevator. As she pushed the button for the third floor, a young man called out for her to hold the elevator. Torrey didn't move, she wasn't willing to risk dropping her things in an attempt to press the open-door button. Hell, another elevator would open for him once she was gone.

Dashing through the elevator doors just in time, the young man looked at Torrey and remarked, "Dang, you were just going to let the doors close on me. That's cold."

"Well, as you can see, my arms are full, so…"

"I know, I was just messing with you," He smiled warmly. "May I help you with your things?"

"No thanks, I'm good," Torrey replied.

The elevator stopped on three and Torrey exited. Surprisingly, the young man exited behind her and began following her down the hall. She wasn't familiar with him and she started to get a little freaked out as he continued to follow a few paces behind. She gripped her keys and decided to stop at one of the neighboring doors to see if he would keep walking. But as soon she stopped, so did he.

"Are you sure you're at the right door, ma'am?"

"Why are you following me?" Torrey asked anxiously.

"Lady, I'm not following you, I'm just trying to go home. You're standing in front of my door," He responded calmly.

Torrey felt incredibly foolish. Hanging her head, she sheepishly replied, "I'm sorry, I thought that condo was still unoccupied."

"Sorry to disappoint you, but I moved in a little over a week ago."

Embarrassed, she continued her journey down the hall. He watched from his open door as she unlocked and entered her condo three doors down. He couldn't help but smile as she disappeared into her place.

The night was uneventful. No winds blew, no storm surges took over the city. Torrey spent the evening catching up on work emails and reading her book club's book of the month. After a couple of glasses of wine and a few book chapters, Torrey

shut the lights off and drifted off into a peaceful slumber. It wasn't until the five

o'clock hour that she began to wake at the sounds of the wind and rain. She reached

for the television remote and began to listen to the news broadcasters as they warned

of the dangerous winds and potential for floods.

"If you are still in the city, we urge you to stay where you are," The anchor

woman continued to give warnings and instructions.

Torrey quickly jumped in the shower and dressed for the day. In case something

did go wrong, she didn't want to be the one getting rescued in a night gown and head

wrap. As the hours crept by, the winds grew stronger and the rain began pounding the

building. Torrey continued to watch the local news as she sipped her coffee and

munched on a bagel. She stood from the table and ventured to the window. Just as

she peeked out, a huge tree branched fell onto an electrical pole and the transformer

sparked and crackled. Torrey jumped back and was suddenly without power.

"Damn, maybe I should've gone back to Vidalia," She mumbled as she watched

the power lines fall to the streets.

The storm raged on for hours and Torrey could only light candles as the daylight

gave way to dusk. Periodically, she'd check her phone for live Facebook video

updates from Savannah's Alderman, Van Johnson. He was always a good source for

information and today was no different. He advised that the power outages were wide spread and that a city curfew was in full effect. But Torrey had no intentions of going anywhere anyway. Then suddenly a tree branch came crashing through her window and Torrey let out a horrific scream. She stood frozen as rain began to blow into her condo. It was the pounding on her door that snapped her out of her shock induced trance. Torrey ran to the door and flung it open to find the neighbor from the elevator standing there.

"I heard you scream, are you okay?" He asked as he looked around and saw the tree branch in the window. "Oh hell, I'll be right back." He ran to his place and came right back with a piece of plywood. Not waiting for an invitation to come in, he dashed past Torrey, pushed the branch out of the window and boarded up the hole.

"Thank you so much!" Torrey exclaimed. "Oh my gosh, that scared the crap out of me. I don't know what I would've done had you not run to my rescue. Thank you... Oh wow, I don't even know your name."

"Maxwell, my name is Maxwell. And you are?"

"I'm Torrey, Maxwell and if you wait a second I'll get you a towel." She dashed down the hall and came back with a plush bath towel. "Here you go, use this to dry off."

"Thank you, Torrey. Aside from the window, are you okay?"

"Yes, I'm fine now," She giggled. "I'm just going to light a few candles, fix some dinner, and wait out the storm.

"I was about to do the same. What are you having?" Maxwell asked in a silky baritone voice. A voice Torrey hadn't paid any attention to until now.

"Well, I'm going to make a very fine PB&J sandwich which will be paired with a lovely glass of white wine," she teased. "Would you like to join me? The least I can do is feed you after the way you ran to my rescue."

"How about you put on some shoes, grab the wine, and join me at my place. My dinner is going to be a little more sophisticated." Sensing her hesitation, he tilted his head and spoke softly, teasingly. "I've got a cooler full of ice and lobster salad. Salad that's going to taste pretty amazing on the fresh baked rolls I pulled out of the oven before the lights went out."

"Let me get my shoes," Torrey said without hesitation. She grabbed her phone, keys, wine and dashed out the door with Maxwell.

After they devoured the lobster salad, they spent the evening drinking wine and getting to know one another. With every word he spoke, Torrey's admiration grew for the man who was six years her junior. Not only was he handsome, but the twenty-eight-year-old was a successful architect who had hopes of opening his own firm one day. He was equally impressed with Torrey. Though she made a big deal about their age difference, he loved her confidence and admired the fact that she chose to spend her life serving the youth as an elementary school principle.

167

"I guess I'd better get back to my place," Torrey said as she stood to her feet. "It's super late and I'm getting sleepy."

"Or you could just crash here," Maxwell offered. "The power is still out, it's still raining and I'm really enjoying your company." He stepped closer to Torrey, took her face in his hands, kissed her forehead and said, "Please stay."

Torrey wasn't sure if it was the wine, how attractive he was, the fact that he ran to her rescue, or the fact that she hadn't been with anyone in almost a year, but she allowed the kiss that he then planted on her lips. She allowed the kisses to grow more passionate. She allowed his hands to roam her body, to discover where she liked to be touched. She not only allowed, but fully participated in the journey to his bed. He peeled her clothes off and she threw her head back in ecstasy as he took her breasts into his mouth. First one and then the other. Her delight only grew as he feasted on all that her body had to offer. In one smooth motion, he slid a condom on and slowly entered her love. His movement literally took her breath away. They wrapped themselves in each other the way that lovers do, until they were both fully satisfied.

"So, what happens after the storm?" Torrey asked, but her question went unanswered. She wasn't sure if Maxwell had fallen asleep or if he simply chose to remain silent and make no promises that he had no intention of keeping.

The blaring of music jolted the pair out of their sleep. It was seven in the morning, the storm had ceased and the electricity was back on. Torrey and Maxwell faced each other, but neither spoke. Torrey got up and dressed, gathered her things and simply said goodbye.

Two hours later, Torrey heard a knock at her door. She looked through the peep hole and saw Maxwell with some strange man. She hesitantly opened the door. "Hey, what are you doing here?"

"This is a friend of mine who's in the window business. He's going to replace that broken window." Maxwell said as he nodded his head toward the covered hole.

Torrey watched as the gentleman made his way into her place and began to work. "Maxwell, you didn't have to do this. I was just about to call my insurance company, so they could send someone out."

"Don't bother, I've got it all handled. That's what men do after the storm. They take care of what's broken."

Torrey smiled, "Is that all that they do?"

"Oh no, that's just where they start. After the storm is the time for new beginnings. It's when flowers and relationships blossom. After the storm is when I start loving you."

For A Lifetime

Adam walked into the restaurant and surveyed the room as he anxiously waited for the hostess to seat him. It had been six years since he'd enjoyed the ambiance and various culinary delights. Finally, the hostess asked him to follow her and he gladly did. Just as he'd requested, he was seated at a small, dimly lit, corner table. Adam placed his drink order and patiently waited to find out why he'd been summoned to the place that held his greatest heartache.

Seven and a half years ago, Adam met Sharla at her family's restaurant. She was the hostess at the time and as soon as he laid eyes on her, he knew she was the one. When he first asked her out on a date, she shot him down without a second thought. But Adam was not deterred, he went back every night, sat at the same table, and tried to engage her in conversation. Sharla was courteous, after all, it was her job to be. However, as the days went on, Sharla found herself laughing at Adam's corny jokes. She was flattered each time he'd bring her flowers, and called him a suck up each time he gave flowers to her mother. Sharla's parents thought that he was the perfect guy for her. Her father declared that Adam's persistence spoke to his good heart and pure intentions. After two weeks of restaurant visits, Sharla finally agreed to go out on a date with Adam.

A year and a half later found Adam ready to propose. For him, it had been a love at first sight situation. Yes, it had taken Sharla a longer period of time to develop sincere and honest feelings for Adam. For some unknown reason, she felt that with him she'd always be missing out on something better. When he was sure that she'd finally let go of that notion and loved him for the man that he was, he purchased a flawless, two karat diamond ring. Sharla's family had shut the restaurant down for the evening, filled the venue with candles, champagne, and an elegant violinist. The stage was set for the perfect proposal. But sadly, when Sharla arrived, she walked in with the intention to dissolve their relationship. Adam was blindsided by her declaration of love for another man.

"I'm sorry, Adam, but Quincy fills my life with excitement. Every day with him is a thrill. Please know that I never wanted to hurt you, but I learned a long time ago that people come into our lives for a reason, a season, or a lifetime. No offense, but we were seasonal, and our season is over." With that, Sharla trotted back out the door, jumped into Quincy's car and was gone.

All that happened six years ago. Quincy never married Sharla, he had fun with her and then their season ended. Adam had thought of her often, but had no desire to see her until her mother tracked him down and practically begged him to come by for a visit. Now he sat in the corner, watching everyone enjoy their meals. His head turned every time someone came through the door, hoping it would be Sharla. Then it happened, a woman with the face of an angel emerged from the kitchen. She was much thinner than he remembered and wore a scarf on her head. She stood for a moment and looked around. After a few seconds, her mother stepped up, took her by the arm, and escorted her to Adam's table.

"I saw you the moment you stepped in the door," Her mother said. We've missed you so much, Adam and I'm glad to see you still looking well." After she planted a kiss on his cheek, she helped Sharla to sit and left the ex-lovers alone.

"It's so good to see you," Sharla confessed.

After an exchange of pleasantries, Sharla told Adam about her illness. How she was diagnosed with cancer eight months ago. The chemo had left her weak and frail, but thankfully she'd just finished her last treatment. Adam's heart broke a little more with each word she spoke. As much as he'd tried to deny it, he still loved her.

"This battle has taught me the value of real love and it has shown me how flawed and foolish I was. I honestly have no expectation of you forgiving me, but I must apologize. I'm so very sorry for deceiving you, for not loving you the way that you loved me. I'm sorry for my lack of appreciation for you. You are an amazing man,

172

Adam, and I'm sorry that I didn't recognize that earlier and reciprocate your love when I had the chance."

"All I ever wanted was for you to recognize me for the lifetime person that I was in your life. Sharla, I've always been your lifetime."

Three months later, Sharla's cancer was in remission and she was feeling better than she had in years. She also felt more loved than she imagined she ever could. Her slow stroll down the aisle towards her groom, Adam, was proof that forgiveness is possible, and love does conquer all.

~~~

When she was first diagnosed with cancer, the doctors warned Sharla that the treatment might very well leave her infertile. She hadn't thought much about it then, to her the cure was worth any side effects or consequences. That was then, but after she and Adam married, fertility became a very important issue.

"Baby, I love you. Whether we're able to conceive or not, I love you and we're going to be fine," Adam reassured her.

Tears in her eyes, Shayla sniffed and cried, "A woman that can't bear a child is not a real woman."

Adam pulled his wife into his arms. "Sharla, your body's ability to release an egg does not determine your womanhood. You are an amazingly strong, beautiful, sexy as hell woman. You're my woman, my lifetime woman." He lovingly kissed her forehead and wiped her tears.

Time went on and the couple continued to build a beautiful life together. They'd purchased a new home, Adam's career was advancing faster than he ever imagined it would, and Sharla had started a successful blog focusing on women's health. But still she longed for a baby and felt it was time to take a new path in their quest to become parents. She'd contacted an adoption agency and hoped to discuss what she'd learned with Adam over dinner.

Adam arrived home to succulent aromas wafting through the air and a beautifully set, candle lit dining table. As soon as he closed the door, Sharla ran to great him like an excited child that wanted their parent's attention.

"Welcome home, love," She sang as she threw her arms around his neck. "I have a surprise for you. Come on in, wash up, and I'll tell you about it over dinner."

"I have a surprise for you too, babe," Adam grinned as he put his briefcase down and followed Sharla's instructions.

As they began to partake of the delicious meal, Sharla pulled out the information she'd received from the adoption agency. All Adam saw was a picture of a baby and a broad smile planted itself on his face.

"Babe, I think we have the same surprise for each other." He grabbed his briefcase and pulled out a small CVS bag.

"Adam, why would you buy me a pregnancy test? That's just hurtful," Sharla cried.

"Sharla, baby breathe," He instructed as he took his wife's hand in his. "Let me ask you, when was your last cycle?"

"What do you mean? It was last month…I think." Confusion covered her face as she tried to remember exactly when her last period was.

"Sharla, it's been almost two months since you had a cycle. I know the doctor said that it was a long shot, but I really think you may be pregnant. Please just go take the test. As a favor to me, please."

Five minutes later, Sharla emerged from the bathroom carrying a slightly wet pregnancy stick with a bright blue plus sign on it. They laughed, cried, and praised God. The next day, Sharla made an emergency appointment with her OB/GYN physician. Adam promised to meet her there. He wanted to be present for every step of the pregnancy.

Forty-five minutes into the appointment and Adam still hadn't arrived. Sharla tried calling his phone multiple times, but to no avail. Frustrated, she left and returned home, only to be greeted by the police.

"We're so sorry, ma'am. The tractor trailer veered into his lane and forced him into the median wall."

It was too much for Sharla to process. She collapsed to the ground.

~~~

Sharla had cried what seemed like a million tears. The very thought of raising their child without Adam was more than she could bear. Her parents had been by her side since the accident and were a constant source of strength. Sharla was grateful for them and took everything that they had to give emotionally. She knew that all they transferred to her, she'd have to transfer to Adam. While she was thankful that God had spared his life, she dreaded the moment that she'd have to hold his hand while the doctors told him that they weren't able to save his leg.

The doctors had never seen anything like it. Adam took the news of his leg being amputated with the courage of a warrior. He was determined to be walking as normally as possible by the time he and Sharla's baby was born. Adam worked intently with the physical therapists and was only days away from being fit with a prosthetic.

"Baby, I know that when we married you had no thoughts of being with a disabled person. I know this is a lot to take in. Please don't be afraid to tell me if it's too much," Adam said as he readied himself to hear what could be a devastating declaration from Sharla.

Sharla positioned herself in front of Adam. She wanted to assure him that she was all in and what better way to do that than to make love to him. She unbuckled his pants, but as he lifted his body to remove them, a wave of nausea came over her. She jumped up and ran for the restroom where she emptied her stomach. There was no love making that night or any other for the next month. Try as he might, Adam couldn't help but feel that it was because of his leg, or lack thereof.

As Sharla's pregnancy advanced, so did Adam's strength and ability to move freely with his prosthetic leg. He hadn't bothered to ask Sharla any further questions about their relationship or her feelings toward his disability. In his heart, he knew that this was not what she wanted. Sharla wanted, desired, craved a whole man and not a fake bionic man. His decision was made, Adam would look for and move into his own place within the week.

Sharla had absolutely no idea that Adam had a million negative thoughts swirling around in his head. All she knew was that all the illness she'd been feeling had finally dissipated and had been replaced with feelings of lust. That night, she watched as Adam undressed. She licked her lips as she admired his now bulging muscles. When he disappeared behind the bathroom door, Sharla jumped up, grabbed a maternity negligee, and wiggled her pregnant belly into it. She situated herself as seductively as possible on the bed.

Adam was completely surprised to see his wife dressed as she was with an alluring look in her eyes. Had he been wrong about her? Had he allowed his own insecurities to make him withdraw from her? The way she made love to him that night proved that he had done just that. Adam had misjudged everything. That night, Sharla replaced all of his doubts and insecurities with love, pure, beautiful love.

Five months later, the happy couple welcomed a perfect bundle of joy. Their little girl, Ayana, was a dream made real and so was the little boy they welcomed seventeen months after her birth. Everything was finally perfect…then the phone rang.

~~~

Adam walked in the door to find his daughter trying to comfort her crying mother as best any toddler could. When Sharla called Adam crying uncontrollably, his first thought was that the doctor had called with the results from her latest biopsy and the news wasn't good. Seeing the state she was in, he was sure that his assumption was right. But just as she had seen him through his crisis, he would do the same for her. He rushed to her side and began to tell her that they would get through this together.

"Baby, between our faith in God and man's medicine, you'll beat this cancer again. We'll beat it because I will be with you every step of the way. I love you baby."

"I love you too, Adam, but it's not cancer, it's much worse. Mama had a massive heart attack. I've called the babysitter and she's on her way over so that we can go to the hospital. Daddy is there alone and he says that it doesn't look good.," She sobbed.

Before Adam could respond, the doorbell rang. He showed the sitter in, grabbed his wife's purse, and ushered her out to the car.

"Adam, she has to make it. I won't make it without my mom. She has been everything to me, my counselor, my nurse, my best friend. I can't lose her now," Sharla wailed.

"Baby, she's a strong woman and God is merciful. He's not going to take her before her time," Adam encouraged her as he whipped through the city streets.

They parked and made it to the cardiac unit in record time. They saw Sharla's dad waiting and nervously wringing his hands. He jumped up when he saw them approaching and pulled his daughter into a tight embrace as soon as she was within reach. He explained to them how she'd been working in the restaurant as usual, but started complaining about back pain and being unusually tired. He told her to sit and rest, but before she could make it to a chair, she gripped her arm and fell to the floor.

A tall, middle aged doctor entered the small waiting room and confirmed that they were the family of Mrs. Patterson. "I am sorry, but it doesn't look good. Mrs. Patterson suffered a massive heart attack and the damage is irreparable."

"Can we please see her?" Sharla sobbed.

The doctor tried to prepare them for all the tubes and machines she was hooked up to as he ushered them into her room. The three of them surrounded her bed, held hands and lifted her in prayer. As they prayed, Mrs. Patterson's eyes fluttered open. She smiled at them and mouthed, "I love you."

Three days later they laid Mrs. Patterson to rest. Sharla was completely heartbroken, but the love of her husband, the support he gave made things more tolerable for her. It wasn't long before her father told her that he was selling the restaurant and moving back to his hometown of Phoenix, Arizona.

"Do you already have a buyer for the restaurant, Dad?"

"No, but I think it'll sell pretty fast. I hate to let it go, but I can't run it alone. It was me and your mom's dream, but without her, the dream dies."

Sharla looked at Adam and he instantly knew what she wanted. He simply nodded at his wife, she smiled, looked at her dad and said, "The dream doesn't have to die. Daddy, let us buy the restaurant? It'll remain in the family, we can continue the work that you and Mama started."

Mr. Patterson embraced his daughter and son-in-law. "This is a dream come true." He reached in a keep sake box that belonged to his wife and pulled out a note. It was written on a recipe card in Mrs. Patterson's hand writing and read, *Lord, let what we've built be a legacy for our family. Let it pass from generation to generation. Bless it as it passes from our hands to theirs.*

The next ten years brought about a lot of change. A third adopted child, the passing of Mr. Patterson, and the expansion of the business. They opened a second location across town and it was just as popular as the first. Even Sharla and Adam's

love changed, it grew deeper and stronger with the passing of each year.